What People Are Saying

"It's about time! I was hooked after the first chapter!"
A. F. Bradley, Founder - Restoring Dignity, Inc.

"Relatable." D. Stone, Regional Sales Director

"Powerful! This book is for the person looking for answers and the person who wants to supply them an answer." Dr. D. Gardner - #1 Best Selling Author on Amazon of *Increase Your Capacity to Hear from God* and *Overcoming the Enemy's Storms*

"Revolutionary! I love the prayer asking God to cover "open places" while He identifies and closes doors open to the enemy." E. Miller-retired Women's National Basketball Association

"Stop! Take time to assess where you are in a relationship. Look! See how this book teaches you to decode a relationship. Listen! Hear and take heed to the wisdom shared." Rev. J. Rudder-Ward, MBA - Founder Positive Image Network, Inc. and Image Maker Vision Communication

BREAK FREE!

Princes and Predators:
Both Treat You Like a Queen
Know the Difference

Gina Marie, M. A.

**Break Free! Princes and Predators: Both Treat You Like a Queen
Know the Difference**

By Gina Marie, M.A.
Copyright © 2020 by Proclaim Publishing

www.GinaMarie.org
Facebook: GinaMarie@GinaMarieBreakFree
Email: Info@ginamarie.org

Cover Design and Layout by: ChristianAuthorsGetPaid.com

Back Cover Photo: Joan Rudder-Ward

Editor: Susan Titus Osborn
Susantosb@gmail.com

Unless otherwise noted, all Scripture quotations are taken from the New King James Version® (NKJV). Copyright © 1982 by Thomas Nelson, Inc. Used by permission. All rights reserved.

Scripture marked KJV are taken from the King James Version. Public domain.

Definitions are sourced from www.miriam-webster.com unless otherwise indicated.

DISCLAIMER:

This is the author's life story, and thus, the information, opinions, and accounts herein represent her personal experience, memories, and perspective about the subjects disclosed and the people involved. She has made every effort to relay the details to the best of her recollection and knowledge. As such, as well as due to the sensitivity of the subject covered in this personal account, names have been changed in the book to protect identities.

Although the author speaks from first-hand experience, she does not assume any liability for any loss, risk, or injury (physical, emotional, mental, or financial) incurred by any individuals mentioned within (whose identities are duly protected) or by those who read the information enclosed.

Printed in the United States of America

ISBN 978-0-578-44081-1

Dedication

This book is dedicated to anyone who has ever had to escape danger and to those that need to.

For I know the thoughts that I think toward you, says the Lord, thoughts of peace and not of evil, to give you a future and a hope.
Jeremiah 29:11

For God has not given us a spirit of fear,
but of power and of love and of a sound mind.
2 Timothy 1:7

Acknowledgements

I would like to acknowledge Dr. Diane Gardner, the trailblazer, and mentor who aggressively encouraged me to record my journey from fear to freedom to show others how to break free. I would also like to acknowledge: Robert, Nairobi, Adrian, Kathleen, Dan, and Susan; my Prosperity Partners Reverend Joan, JoJo, Eugenia, and Lori; my family; and the members of God's House of Favor Church. What a journey! Your unwavering support and steady words of encouragement made this book possible.

I would also like to acknowledge the ministries of Dr. Kenneth C. Ulmer and Dr. Beverly "Bam" Crawford, whose sound teaching helped put me on the path to emotional health.

Table of Contents

Introduction

I pressed a hot washcloth over my face, savoring its warmth against my skin. I applied pressure, slowly wiping in a downward motion. As the cloth passed my eyes, I opened them and caught a glimpse of my reflection in the mirror. I paused. I was in my early 30's. By this time in my life, I had washed my face, rinsed it, and wiped it with a hot washcloth at least 10,950 times. It was routine, not something I had to think about. Yet, this time the routine was interrupted because I did not recognize the woman in the mirror. Of course, I *knew* the reflection was mine. What I mean is, I did not *perceive* who was staring back at me.

Somewhere in the timeline of my life, I lost touch with "Gina." There was a time when I knew who Gina was, what she loved, and what she despised. "Back then," Gina was ever the optimist, staunchly resigned to the belief that the glass is always half-full and not half-empty. Gina loved learning new things and exploring new locations. She enjoyed the sound of the ocean, mountain lodges, the theatre, the bookstore, the beauty of sunsets and nature in general, backgammon, dancing, chocolate chip cookies, and cheering for the underdog. Conversely, Gina despised negativity, bullying, people who take advantage of other people, and the word "can't."

Yet, now, as I looked in the mirror, I could not remember the last time I thought about the things I loved.

My thoughts were littered with how to defend myself from what my boyfriend Myles would say or do. Myles was my second love interest as a young adult. Not only was my mind occupied with thoughts about Myles, but it was also still holding unprocessed trauma from my first love interest Lincoln. Negative words bombarded me. They crashed like storm waves on the shores of my mind. They swept away peace with every ebb and flow. I felt trapped. I wanted desperately to find a way to break free.

I wondered, where was the "me" I once knew? Where was the girl who dreamed of entrepreneurship, education, law, travel, and bilingual communication? Where were the goals I set for myself long ago?

"How did I get here?" I asked myself.

After years of ingesting negative words spoken by two successive love interests I arrived in my thirties, bruised and broken. I was unrecognizable even to my own self.

Negative words spoken by teachers, family and friends were operating—unchecked—in my life for as long as I could remember. Those words were designed to destroy my self-esteem until I no longer had a voice. As I looked in the mirror that day, I realized that the words fulfilled their intended purpose.

God performed the greatest miracle in my life when He taught me my value and healed my orphaned heart. In doing so, He enabled me to hear and embrace the truth. Today, I stand and speak with a bold, new voice after years of shrunken silence. Moreover, I bear those who treated me poorly no animosity.

"How much more shall the blood of Christ, who through the eternal Spirit offered Himself without spot to God, cleanse your conscience from dead works to serve the living God?" (Hebrews 9:14.)

This book details the account of verbal and physical abuse I endured because I did not know the difference between a predator and a prince. It shows how I learned to discern princes from predators and how I rediscovered my own voice. It exposes mindsets that lead to a harmful mental state and, in turn, shows you how to transform your thinking. You will learn to dismantle negative words from the past that still reign in your thoughts. In addition, you will learn how to deflect negative words from the present that do not edify you.

This book is the story of my journey from broken and bruised to *beautiful!* I wrote it to help you find your way to freedom. I long to see tears turn to triumph and victim mindsets transformed into victory. If I could be anything, I would be an agent of change, filled with wisdom to put an end to violence especially, against women. Today I am finally *bold!* Today I am finally *free!* If one woman finds her way to freedom through my testimony, then writing this book will be one of the best things I ever did.

Part One

The Path to Predation

Disturbed by a Dream

In my dream, I was in my room, asleep in my bed. As I was lying there, I began to struggle to keep the tip of my tongue from curling back toward my throat. I tried to lay my tongue flat by pushing it toward my front teeth, but I could not stop the curling movement. I thought I was choking.

I woke up in the middle of the night, gripped with fear! I realized the dream was real! *What is happening?* I shouted in my mind. My tongue felt swollen and heavy, and it was still moving uncontrollably in a curling motion toward the back of my throat. I sat straight up in bed, forcibly trying to uncurl my tongue from the back of my mouth and throat.

I have got to breathe! I thought.

Determined, I clutched my throat. I focused intently on pressing my tongue against my teeth, but it refused to respond. How could I not control the movement of my own tongue? Desperately, I struggled to regain control. I knew time was passing; yet, I could not stop the curling force. Anguished, I screamed silently, *No!*

Then, the sensation stopped as suddenly as it began. Relieved, I took a deep breath. I collapsed back onto the bed. I was baffled and severely shaken over what just happened. The feeling of having my tongue thrust back in my throat and constricting my airway was horrible.

This dream-wake sequence disturbed my sleep for years. It was a regularly recurring phenomenon. After each occurrence, I would lie awake uneasy, and upset. After one occurrence, I remember looking over at Myles. He was sound asleep. I thought,

How could you sleep through that? Surely, you should have been startled awake by all the activity.

I did not understand what was happening. Furthermore, I was deeply troubled over how a dream could seem so real.

Today, I understand the meaning of the dream and would like to share it with you. The dream reflected reality— my actual reality. I was vulnerable, unsuspecting, and in danger of losing my life. The attack in the dream was a warning about the violent nature of the man lying next to me. That man was my boyfriend—Myles.

Like me, you may be trapped, in a bed fighting for your life. A nightmare may plague you and you cannot seem to escape. The "bed" you are lying in is your emotional entanglement with an intimate partner. The "nightmare" is the realization that your partner is not who you thought he was, and you are a prisoner, struggling to survive to your next breath. This is the story of how to recognize the situation, how to get out, and how to overcome it.

Chapter Two

Princes and Predators

A *Prince Charming* is "a suitor who fulfills the dreams of his beloved." A second definition refers to a man of deceptive charm toward women, one who acts like a Prince Charming to get his own way. This person is a predator.

Webster's dictionary defines a *predator* as "an organism that primarily obtains food [benefits] by the killing and consuming of other organisms." It is "an organism that lives by predation." Discerning the difference between princes and predators is the subject of this chapter.

Princes and predators start the same just like the wheat and the tares in the following parable. Matthew 13:24-30, The Parable of the Wheat and the Tares states:

"The kingdom of heaven is like a man who sowed good seed in his field; but while men slept, his enemy came and sowed tares among the wheat and went his way. But when the grain had sprouted and produced a crop, then the tares also appeared. So the servants of the owner came and said to him, 'Sir, did you not sow good seed in your field? How then does it

have tares?' He said to them, 'An enemy has done this.' The servants said to him, 'Do you want us then to go and gather them up?' But he said, 'No, lest while you gather up the tares you also uproot the wheat with them. Let both grow together until the harvest, and at the time of harvest I will say to the reapers, 'First gather together the tares and bind them in bundles to burn them, but gather the wheat into my barn'.'

It is important to note that tares are not weeds. They are counterfeit wheat. They look identical to wheat, but their nature is not nutritive; it is poisonous. Likewise, predators look identical to princes, but their nature is not loving. It is binding. Moreover, tares cannot be distinguished from wheat until "the grain has sprouted and produced a crop." The wisdom of the Scripture is that the plan of the enemy is not known until maturity (the time of reaping). A predator deceives until an appointed time.

Distinguishing between princes and predators is difficult because of their deceptive nature. Seeing through the disguise is even more difficult if you are fixated on being in a relationship or on getting married. **Not** all men are predators. I know many men who are admirable, honorable and forthright. Predators are not gender-specific. Women are not exempt from predatory tactics. Male or female, the intent of a predator is to lure, capture, and devour. The difference between a prince and a predator is defined by the intentions of the heart.

The following stories from my life illustrate the nature of a predator and highlight how they operate— the masks they put on. In doing so, I hope to expose counterfeits that may be operating in your life or in the life of someone you know.

The Pursuit

I met Lincoln, my first adult boyfriend, in my mid-twenties just after I landed my first full-time position in my career and moved into my own apartment. I caught the bus to work to save money for another car. Lincoln drove by, noticed me standing in heels and a career dress, stopped and introduced himself. I was not in the mood to engage in conversation, but I greeted him politely because he was dressed in a military uniform. Lincoln drove by and greeted me in this manner for a series of mornings.

Lincoln was highly skilled in the art of conversation. And he was eventually able to engage me in casual banter as I stood, waiting for the bus. Every day, before the bus came, he offered me a ride, and every day I refused. This went on for several weeks. One morning the weather was particularly cold, wet, and windy and the bus was late. Lincoln offered a ride and I refused, as usual. This time Lincoln persisted and listed all the reasons why taking a ride from him was safe. He stated, "You are standing here waiting for the bus in inclement weather. You know where my office is, and I told you where I live. I am in uniform and driving a government vehicle." He even invited me to check the plates. I peered at the car through the rain and saw the words *US Government* across the license plate and the vehicle number. It was very wet outside. The bus had not arrived. I did not want to be late to work, so I decided to take the chance.

Lincoln delivered me safely to my job at City Hall. After that, I spotted him often near the stores when I got off the bus after work and walked to my apartment. One day he greeted me and asked me for a date. I refused. For several more weeks, he asked me for a date. I refused. Finally, I said that I was busy on all the days he gave me as an option, thinking that this response would stop him from asking me out. Then he said, "How about today?" I was not prepared for that, so I stammered and then agreed.

My criteria for dating at that time were possession of a good job, a car, having one's own place, and being well-dressed. Lincoln was employed by the U.S. government. He was well-dressed. His closet was full of handmade Italian suits. He was tall, handsome and smooth-skinned with a white, winning smile. He had his own means of transportation and his own place. When he showed up at my job he was accompanied by several other marines with flowers in *An Officer and a Gentlemen* fashion. Of course, all of city hall took notice of his grand gesture. After that we dated. For a little while, things were good.

"You Just Don't Listen!"

"You just don't *listen*!" Lincoln spewed vehemently.

I never thought the word "listen" could carry so much hatred. His words were full of venom, and I literally felt sick as if I had ingested poison when I heard them. I closed my eyes, clenched my teeth, and took a deep breath. He was so angry!

I knew I was in trouble. In an earlier conversation, he told me to visit his gym. By the tone of his voice, I knew he also expected me to join his gym. But I found another gym I liked better. I compared the pricing, facilities, classes, location, etc., and determined that what I wanted was found elsewhere. He was *not* happy about it!

I tensed, knowing the onslaught was about to begin. We did not live together, but he spent the night at my place regularly. We were in the bedroom; he was getting dressed for duty. As he put on his socks, he started to list what made *his* gym the better choice.

"My gym is open twenty-four hours," he stated with emphasis.

He put on his sock suspenders to keep his shirt in place and went on, "My gym has the latest equipment," he insisted.

Then, he argued, "There are hidden costs in the membership pricing packages," inferring that I did not understand how to analyze the price options and make a decision. He put on his patent leather shoes, displeasure radiating from his voice.

Next, came a shift in tactics with a barrage of questions. He systematically hurled questions at me, waiting for me to falter in my responses, so he could swoop in for the kill. I felt trapped!

"What type of classes do they have?"

"What are the hours?"

"What type of equipment do they have?"

The barrage continued.

I answered, trying to cover all my bases so I could escape and prove that my decision was a good one. With every answer I gave him, his voice grew louder with the next question he threw at me.

Then one of my answers came out sheepishly with a hint of uncertainty. Smelling blood, he pounced. "See! You just don't listen!"

Exasperated and hurt I responded, "I *do* listen!" In all honesty, I just wanted to scream. I was not guilty. I had done nothing wrong. I looked around for a way to retreat.

But he was still getting dressed and ready for his day. I could not get by him to go out of the bedroom door. Then something unusual happened.

I just stood still. Gazing at him intently as he buttoned his shirt I said, much to my own surprise, "I have the right to make my own decision. Just because I did not choose your gym does not mean I did not listen. It means I did not obey you. Obedience is for children."

A lay counselor with the Encouragers Women's ministry at Faithful Central Church, helped me understand the difference between the verbs listen and obey. What I did not understand is that when he said the word listen, he meant obey: To carry out his direction with no changes. I was able to finally understand that dating someone did not nullify my right to listen, to disagree, and follow my own course of action.

When Lincoln finished buckling his belt, I held my breath and braced myself for his comeback. He reached for his military hat. Without another word, he left the room for duty.

I breathed a sigh of relief. I was safe for now. Remarkably, he never used those words, "You don't listen!" ever again after that incident.

"You Don't Know What Love Is."

Lincoln and I dated for a few years. I suspected that he had not broken things off completely with his ex-girlfriend or that she did not know about me. I decided to date someone else and broke up with Lincoln. I stopped all communication.

One evening I was at home in the living room on the phone when Lincoln called. I ignored it. He called back repeatedly. I would not answer his call. Next there was a knock at my front door, and my doorbell rang. The knock startled me. I realized it was Lincoln.

Lincoln kept ringing the bell, but I would not answer. Then, I heard the front window slide open, and Lincoln stepped over the sill into my living room! I lived on the ground floor of a gated apartment unit. He was angry. He poured himself a glass of water. We argued. He threw water from a glass in my face. I called the police. He left on his own accord.

After that, I called the manager to ask permission to install an alarm and followed through. Lincoln called incessantly and left messages. He called my office phone as well. He even showed up at my job uninvited and unannounced. The men at work offered to call the police and have him removed from the premises. I did not call the police but I protested and set boundaries about showing up at my place of employment. He apologized but switched to letter writing to make his point. He professed undying, love and begged me to give him another chance.

When I finally agreed to meet him, he said, "You don't know what love is because you never had a father." He insisted that his love was genuine and that he wanted to start a family. I pondered those words. He was my first adult relationship. Lincoln had been married before. Maybe I did not know what love was. Maybe this was normal.

I took Lincoln back, based on his commitment to love and start a family. I became pregnant within a few weeks after we reunited. It was a mistake to take him back. Later I understood that he intended to impregnate me so that I would be more dependent on him. He meant to break me like a cowboy breaks the spirit of a free horse and make it difficult for me to survive without support from him.

The Art of War

One night Lincoln and I watched a movie drama about love gone wrong. The actor playing the boyfriend commits some egregious offense in the relationship. The actress playing the girlfriend discovers the offense and promptly decides to kick the boyfriend out of the house and toss his possessions. The boyfriend arrives at their home, ascends the staircase to the door, stepping over piles of his clothes and other possessions strewn on the stairs. He tries to open the door. The locks have been changed, and his key does not work. A yelling match between them takes place with her shouting from the bedroom window and him pleading from the lawn below outside.

After that scene, Lincoln looked at me and remarked that he admired how she stood up for herself, set boundaries, and won the war.

He asked if I knew about the book, *The Art of War*. The book was written in 500 BC and is considered the definitive text on military strategy and warfare. I realized that he viewed relationships like warfare: Know your opponent, do what is unexpected, deceive the enemy, and break the enemy's resistance with systematic control. I remember scoffing and muttering "What a hypocrite!" He tipped his hand. He admired the actresses' actions in the movie, but maligned me if I so much as looked like I would say the word *no*.

Here is the key according to Luke 6:45: *"A good man out of the good treasure of his heart brings forth what is good; and the evil man out of the evil treasure brings forth what is evil; for out of the abundance of the heart his mouth speaks."*

Lincoln's words were true. He *did* admire the fight in me. That is what attracted him to me. But the very thing that attracted him to me is also the very thing he worked to systematically reverse until I possessed no more independent thoughts.

It was a challenge he intended to win. But it was too late. He tipped his hand, and I knew the winning strategy was to stand your ground and fight.

"It's Not Even My Child!"

"It's not even my child!" Lincoln spat.

Lincoln and I were traveling from Los Angeles to Norwalk. His words as we drove were like fists pummeling me. The pain was so sharp and unexpected, it took my breath away.

I put my hands on the dash of the U-Haul van. I put my other hand on my swollen belly. The unborn baby girl in my womb formed a hard ball. Instinctively I breathed out fully to ease the tension and stroked my belly in an effort to comfort her.

I whispered to her, "Everything is going to be okay. Relax, little one. It's okay."

I kept my eyes closed. For the first time, I was painfully aware of how my reactions affected my unborn child. I dug deep, willing myself to find the strength to endure his hateful words.

I was numb from his vicious insult. I could only manage to focus on my breath, determined to be calm for my baby girl, biding my time until I could get free. Silently, I vowed *never* to get into a vehicle—an enclosed space—with him again. I stared out the window, watching the poles go by, giving my mind something to do.

One of Lincoln's favorite tactics was to wait until we were in an enclosed space to start an argument and churn out his verbal assaults. Somehow, I knew if I did not get away from him, I could end up dying a physical death. At the very least, I would die an emotional death, the essence of me gone, stripped by him through his onslaught of hateful words.

I did not want my daughter to grow up in this environment. I found the strength to fight for her even though I would not fight for me. As I fought for her, I found my voice. And I began the journey back to self with a tiny two letter word, *no*. I vowed to get out of this relationship and never look back.

The Elevator

Ding! The elevator doors opened. I was at an office building in Orange County preparing to pay off my car loan. I had a cashier's check for $8,000 to pay for my car and take Lincoln's name off the title. Because the loan was in both of our names his signature was required to transfer title from him to me. This was the last step to severing all ties.

I was feeling confident. My hair, long and thick after giving birth, was swept up in a bun. I was ready.

The elevator for the office building was situated in an atrium. The elevator was made of glass, and it overlooked offices and the atrium. The surrounding offices had a direct line of sight into the elevator as it ascended and descended.

I saw Lincoln waiting for me in the courtyard. As I stepped into the elevator, he stepped in after me. I was occupied with my new cell phone, choosing not to converse with him.

"Nice phone," Lincoln smirked.

The elevator door closed. "It was a birthday gift," I responded. "I bought it for myself," I said proudly.

He taunted, "I should have f***ed you so well."

I was annoyed at his assumption that another man bought the cell phone for me and that he inferred it was because of sexual favors. I scoffed at his remark.

Unexpectedly, Lincoln's hand was around my throat, and my feet were dangling off the elevator floor. I was pinned by the neck up against the elevator wall. The hair I had pinned up so nicely was shaken loose. His grip tightened.

Lincoln was over six feet tall and trained in military combat. I thought, "Is this the end of my life?" I remember thinking that all he had to do was squeeze for it to be over.

Suddenly, the elevator door opened. Still, he held me there a few seconds longer, glaring at me viciously. He then released his grip. I heard the sound of my clothes making contact as I slid down the wall and slumped to the floor. He exited as quickly as he entered.

Moments passed. I heard voices. "Are you alright?" Women who had seen the incident from the office windows came running to my aid. "Oh my God! We saw what happened!"

Another woman ran to get me some water. Tears were pouring down my cheeks. I could not move. I stayed hunched over on the elevator floor.

"We called the police!" another voice said.

The water felt cool and soothing in my throat. "Take my hand," a lady offered gently. "Let's get you to the bathroom."

Kind women helped me put myself back together. When I came outside the bathroom, two policemen were there. One officer asked, "Ma'am, what happened?

I explained that Lincoln grabbed me by the neck.

We can arrest him right now," he offered.

I saw the other officer questioning Lincoln across the courtyard. I didn't know what he was saying about the incident, but I was sure he was not telling the truth. I knew the only way to be rid of him was to cut the final tie that kept us together—the car loan. I also knew if I had him arrested, it would prolong breaking that financial tie. Desperate to be free, I gave up my right to punish his offense.

"I have a check for $8,000. All I need is an escort upstairs to pay off my car loan," I replied. I showed the officer the cashier's check and the payoff paperwork.

The police escorted Lincoln and I to the finance office. The paperwork was signed, legally releasing me from any obligatory tie. As soon as our business was complete, Lincoln took off, passed the officers still livid with me. The officers asked me again if I wanted to press charges. What I really wanted was to just be done with Lincoln. I declined and walked away free from financial and romantic encumbrances and I felt happy.

Chapter Three

Redux

Though I was able to sever emotional ties with Lincoln, the next man I dated had the same predatory nature as the first! In fact, the second dating relationship was more dangerous than the first. Earlier, I shared my vivid, reoccurring dream. The dream began when I met Myles. It continued throughout our dating and ceased as soon as we broke up. I know now that the attack in the dream mirrored the dangerous situation I was in. It was dangerous because I had no knowledge that I was entangled with another predator. I believed that my first relationship was an isolated incident. I had not yet applied the knowledge and obtained wisdom. I did not see the pattern. I had not done the work it takes to heal my emotions from trauma and build my self-esteem. This is the story of my second encounter with a predator.

Myles was my second adult relationship. When I met Myles, he possessed all the trappings of a modern-day prince or what I call the 5 C's: clothes, culture, car, charisma, and cash.

Myles was always well groomed. He did *not* step out of the house until he was resplendent, his manner of dress impeccable. In fact, I did not know Nordstrom's and Macy's had a separate men's store until I met Myles.

Besides designer clothing, he also had an extensive collection of colognes. Visiting the fragrance bar with him was how I learned about the necessity of coffee beans when testing colognes and perfumes. Smelling coffee beans refocuses the nose so that you can smell a fragrance one after the other.

From traveling with Myles, I also learned about the concierge level at fine hotels that could only be accessed with a separate elevator key. This entire floor is dedicated to special services and upgrades.

Myles loved fast, foreign, luxury means of transportation. He drove high-end models of luxury vehicles. The Lexus was his everyday car, but the Mercedes Benz, two-door sports coupe was his favorite.

Myles was independently wealthy. He was an entrepreneur from New York and did not work your typical 9-5 job. Myles was a self-described black sheep of his family compared to his older siblings. They were very successful in corporate America. His brother was a vice president of a premier media company, his sister was a psychiatrist, and his mom was the head of a successful, non-profit foundation. Flush with money, he always had stacks of $100 bills in his wallet and more stacks of cash in his home safe. Sharing a home with his sister, he lived in a Southern California suburb where the average household income was above six figures. He looked and lived the part of a prince, possessing all the outward charm you would expect of royalty.

And Myles treated me like a queen. In fact, the first time I saw him, I was walking with a co-worker to grab some lunch. He announced to my co-worker, "You are walking with a queen!" While with him, I dined at upscale restaurants, traveled to museums, and aquariums, and took tours of historic sights. I had never experienced the travel and shopping lifestyle he took for granted.

He purchased pricey, designer gifts for me. The first gift was a Tag Heuer watch for Christmas. The price tag on the watch was equivalent to a mortgage payment because of the sapphire crystal watch face versus a glass watch face and meter depth. This was all new to me. The watch I wore was a Timex. I remember feeling uneasy about the gift given the price and the newness of our relationship. When I questioned Myles about it, he replied "Aren't you worth it?" He continued to give me gifts that made a statement. For graduation he gave me a Mont Blanc pen, and on another occasion a Coach handbag.

I discovered that like Lincoln, Myles was *not* a prince. Although he attended church every Sunday and could quote the Bible verbatim, he lacked the sixth and most important "C" that a prince needs—*character*. Like the wheat and the tares, princes and predators may be indistinguishable from the other until time reveals the true nature of the person. At maturity, there is no "fruit" on the tare. No character. The following accounts illustrate how Myles operated behind closed doors, and the tools he used to manipulate.

Handpicked

I did not know Myles handpicked me from the moment he saw me. Our dates were a series of innocent outings to bookstores, a Bible study group, dinners, and long walks on the beach. Yet unbeknownst to me, these "dates" were actually calculated interviews. Myles learned everything he needed to know about me, and he used the information to his advantage. That is the mark of a predator.

Unfortunately, I had not yet learned the wisdom of discretion. As a result, I freely shared all my hopes, dreams, and fears with him. When Myles heard a fact from my life that aligned with a fact from his life, he pointed out the common denominators and used them to establish a point of agreement between us. He portrayed himself as being just like me. For example, he was a single man with a daughter in

New York and an infant son in Southern California. I had an infant daughter. He talked about his struggles with his son's mother, and I shared my communication struggles with my daughter's dad. We bonded over these areas of commonality.

I had not learned my value or self-worth back then. I felt compassion for him given our similar situations with significant others. It was easy to make an emotional connection.

From Complimentary to Cruelty

At first, Myles was complimentary of everything I accomplished and my perspective on life. Exactly when the tide turned from complimentary to critical to cruel is difficult to pinpoint. It was subtle and slow. Over time, the verbal darts increased in frequency. The topics were not isolated or related to any specific trigger. Anything was fair game. Daily, I ingested poisonous words about my appearance, flaws on my skin, my clothes, my hair, how I kept house, how I cooked and how I parented my daughter. *Everything*. Nothing was sacred or off limits to his criticism and verbal assaults.

Critical and cruel words are like poison. Eating poison is gambling with death—either a slow death from consistently ingesting small, daily doses or a sudden death from a large and lethal dose. Myles administered daily doses of verbal poison. If I asserted myself, he would attack. And I was slowly dying inside.

Spiritual Abuse

Spiritual abuse is using Bible passages to control or manipulate. Myles' favorite Scripture was Proverbs 21:9: *"Better to dwell in a corner of a housetop than in a house with a contentious woman."* I definitely did not want to be accused of being contentious, so I refrained from voicing any opinion opposite of his.

His second favorite Scripture was Ephesians 5:22: *"Wives, submit to your own husbands, as to the Lord."* Three things are noteworthy about Myles's interpretation of this Scripture. First, I was not his wife and not required to submit. He wanted a shortcut, to enjoy the benefits of a wife at a bargain—without covenant and commitment. It was a brilliant plan. Myles kept telling me, "You will never be married!" Upon hearing these words my "fix-it" meter went into over-drive. I earnestly wanted to be a wife, so I submitted to his demands, determined to prove I was wife material. It never occurred to me that he was not husband material.

Second, he interpreted the word *submit* to mean submissive and subservient. Geographically he interpreted submit to mean a place that is under or beneath. Under is not the rightful place of a wife in a covenant relationship with a husband. Her rightful position is alongside him. Three times Scripture says that a husband shall cleave to his wife:

Genesis 2:24 (KJV): *"Therefore shall a man leave his father and his mother, and shall cleave unto his wife: and they shall be one flesh."*

Matthew 19:4-5(KJV): *"For this cause shall a man leave father and mother, and shall cleave to his wife, and they two shall be in one flesh."*

Ephesians 5:25 (KJV): *"Husbands, love your wives, just as Christ also loved the church and gave Himself for her."*

A husband cannot cleave to a wife that is lying underneath his foot. For the grabber to successfully cleave or grab a hold of the *grabee*, requires an upright position rather than a prostrate position. Moreover, it implies that the 'grabee' is moving quickly as opposed to standing still lest there is no need to grab—a simple hand to the shoulder would suffice.

Finally, Myles's interpretation of Ephesians 5:22 conflicts with Ephesians 5:25 which gives the following instruction to husbands: *"Husbands love your wives as Christ loved the church."*

Cleary, Myles did not love me as Christ loved the church. Dr. Kenneth C. Ulmer taught a message entitled "For Women Only" during which he shared a truth I will never forget. Until I understood the godly meaning of submission, the word *submit* literally held me in bondage. Dr. Ulmer shared this truth, "I never met a wife who had a problem submitting to a husband who was submitted to Christ!" Once I learned this truth, Myles was never able to use that tactic again.

Marking Territory

Myles pressured me incessantly for a key to my place. I refused. Soon Myles was "over" at my place all the time, claiming more and more territory with each visit. It started with a toothbrush "inadvertently" left in the bathroom drawer. A t-shirt appeared, folded on the dresser. One article of dry-cleaning showed up, hanging in my closet. He never asked permission if he could leave something behind. He simply, yet forcibly, marked his territory within my own home. After he accused me of dating someone else, I eventually acquiesced and gave him a key to prove that I was not dating anyone else. He continued to maintain a separate residence, whenever I did not measure up to his standards, which changed *all* of the time. He would leave and return to his own residence as "punishment" for my behavior.

Frozen

Myles turned on the air conditioning one day when we were on the road. I complained that the air was too cold and asked if he would turn it down. Instead of turning it down, Myles turned the air on full blast. Halfway through the trip, he took note of my refusal to make a remark about the air.

He set the temperature to the lowest possible setting and even colder air continued to stream through the vents. He left the air on for the duration of the hour and a half trip from L.A. to my house.

I knew this was a test. And that I would lose the battle if I broke down and begged him to turn it off. Normally I run for a blanket or turn up the heat the second the temperature is nippy. I could feel the cold air in my bones, and I shivered.

I found the strength to endure the cold. A few minutes before we arrived at the house, he retreated first and turned the air off. I remember being surprised because he was ever the aggressor. For Myles, exerting dominance and bullying was a way of life ingrained into his behavior.

Exhibitionist

One evening after church, Myles and I were on the road traveling back to my house from Los Angeles. Now, Myles was prone to speed. Rather, I should say he was prone to exhibitionist-style, dangerous driving well over the speed limit. I agonized over each car ride home because of the dangerous way Myles operated the vehicle. Not only would he speed, but Myles would race other drivers on the freeway with me in the car.

As we drove to my house one night, another vehicle sped past us, crashing into the center median. A young lady was thrown from the vehicle across the freeway lanes. We stopped to tend to her until the paramedics arrived. I realized how quickly speeding could turn to tragedy. Myles had a habit of racing with other vehicles on the open road with no regard for his life or that of his passengers. The reality call was enough to help me find the strength to tell Myles that his speeding was intolerable, dangerous, and selfish, and that I would never get into the vehicle with him again.

"Oh, I Thought You Left Those There for Me!"

Be warned! Allowing your partner to receive mail at your house establishes residency no matter whose name is on the lease or deed.

Many nights, I called the police—and the locksmith. Anything to restrict Myles's access and maintain some control. When the police arrived, all Myles had to do was show them a piece of mail with his name on it and the keys and he was allowed to stay.

One night, he called after being freshly kicked out. He said, "I left something of Conner's [his son] in the room." I would not have let him enter for something of his. I was not prepared for his seemingly innocent plea to retrieve an item for his infant son that he left behind. Caving to his plea, I agreed to let him return to fetch the toy.

When he entered, I accompanied him to the room. He headed right for the bed and reached under it to retrieve Connor's toy. Truth hit me suddenly. I mused. "Why didn't he search though drawers, or in the closet or move furniture or pillows to find the toy?"

It was true. Something had been left in the room. What was *not* true was why it was left. The intent behind his request was not innocent. I assumed he left it inadvertently in his haste to pack up and leave. What I did not suspect was the lengths that Myles would go through to preserve access. The reality was, he purposely planted his son's toy, so he would have cause to enter my home again.

Hear me when I say that once a violent partner is out, he *will* try to return with a vengeance! It is truly unbelievable the lengths that an abuser will go through to regain "lost" territory.

The set of keys I took from him were still on a shelf in the living room. He exited the room and stepped into the hallway with his son's toy. He stood waiting for me to say something. I made no effort to engage in conversation nor did I invite him to stay for a short while. He saw the keys and picked them up. When I protested, he responded saying, "Oh! I thought you left those there for me!" I emphatically told him to put the keys back where they were and bid him good night.

How presumptuous to assume that letting him back in to retrieve a toy meant that full access was restored.

"Everything She Has Is Because of Me!"

After one explosive, nocturnal battle of wills, a girlfriend of mine came to my rescue. She confronted Myles about his behavior. He said something that night I have never forgotten. "Everything she has is because of me!"

My girlfriend retorted, "Surely you cannot take credit for her degree, her career, her salary, her place. You are not paying the rent. She is! It's *her* name on the lease. If she wants you out, you need to get f*** out!"

Suddenly, I realized my girlfriend's response was the truth. I spent so much time defending myself from his accusations, I forgot how much I brought to the table. I forgot who I was.

Daily Drama

In that season, I found no solace. I had a career in land use development. I used my analytical, writing, and presentation skills all day long. After work, I picked up my infant daughter from her caregiver, cooked a full meal, made lunch for the next day, and cleaned the house spotless. Then I argued with Myles on the phone or, when he spent the night, in person until the pre-dawn hours of the morning. I would awake the next day exhausted, both physically and mentally, and repeat the cycle all over again.

When asked to share what my life was like during ministry events, I said, "Drama was regularly on the menu. We ate it for breakfast, lunch, and dinner!" The question I pondered in between arguments is "How did I go from the frying pan into the fire?" Even though I was able to leave my first adult relationship with Lincoln, I still chose Myles as a second boyfriend with the same predatory characteristics!

"He Put Hands on Me!"

I moved from an apartment into my first home while dating Miles. One evening, I was prepping a meal and getting ready for the next day. Although Myles lived elsewhere, he had a key to the new house I just purchased and he let himself in. A conversation took place between us that night. I remember disagreeing with him, and in the next instant, I was picking myself up off the hallway floor.

It happened so fast. I stumbled my way to the bathroom. The imprints of his hands were on my skin, and the pain from the impact set in and throbbed. Hot tears ran down my cheeks. The eyes of the image staring back at me were hauntingly lifeless.

The escalation of violence from words to physical assault came suddenly like an earthquake with no warning. I examined myself carefully after the attack. My shirt was ripped, and large welts were on my arms. I was in complete shock. *I can't believe he hit me!* my mind screamed.

He told me he hit and kicked his former girlfriend, but he had never hit or kicked *me*. Because I believed his side of the story, I did not think it would ever happen to me.

The Single State of Mind

At thirty, I believed a woman with a career bore a stigma if she did not have a husband. Access to upper management in my career was off limits to an unmarried woman. The unspoken judgment that stigmatized me was: "If she can't make a relationship work then how can she run a division?" To top it off, everyone I knew was married, and I was tired of flying solo.

I sought marriage instead of enjoying being me. I did not yet understand the wisdom of learning who you are and the importance of being comfortable and confident in your overall health and well-being.

Social media and our culture portray premarital partnerships as a normal step toward marriage or in place of marriage altogether (common-law). Far be it from me to cast judgment. Accusations about premarital/common-law relationships only make the people in those relationships defensive. My purpose in bringing up the subject is to focus on the *emotional state* of a woman in a premarital partnership.

Being unmarried and in an intimate relationship is the most emotionally vulnerable position a woman can find herself in because the one thing you desire above all else is to be "emotionally covered" by your partner. To be emotionally covered in an intimate relationship is to have the security that someone has your back as a loving partner in a permanent and committed way.

Being covered is the one thing you cannot get when involved in a premarital relationship. This state leaves room for feelings of inadequacy and insecurity to stack up higher and higher every day you stay in the relationship without the desired outcome. Remaining in the partnership in hopes of attaining the emotional covering "someday"—one that is provided only through a good, solid, and committed marriage— is like a mule hitched to a cart that is being lured with a carrot tied to a stick to keep it moving. In the end, you spend your days toiling for a carrot you can never obtain. If a man is involved with you intimately without the covenant of marriage, he is using you. Just like the mule, you will follow the carrot he dangles in front of you—believing the hopes and dreams for the future he *appears* to promise. Being in this type of relationship is a dangerous game of strategy, one that constantly had me on edge while I strived to please him. To be honest, I did not want to go through the stigma of being alone. Therefore, I justified Myles' behavior. Plainly put, justifying involves lying to yourself about the truth. I was in love with his prince potential rather than who he actually was. Not all partners are predators. But all partners who want the pleasure of sexual intimacy without commitment lack courage and honor.

The Four I's:

Idolize, Isolate, Invent, Introduce

There are four, progressive stages a predator utilizes to gain control: *Idolize, Isolate, Invent and Introduce*. After stage four, if a victim stays in the relationship, then one of the following is true:

1. They do not know how to get out.
2. They are afraid to get out.
3. They do not want to go through the amount of change it will take to get out.

In the first stage, a predator **idolizes** the victim. The victim can do no wrong. The abuser turns on the charm to establish a strong, emotional attachment. When I first met Myles, he was full of compliments about my education, my career, and my entrepreneurial mindset. Sadly, nurturing words of encouragement were non-existent in my formative years. In fact, I was a grown woman before I ever heard my adoptive mother say, "I love you." Naturally, then, these compliments met a deep need within me to feel loved and appreciated. Myles was openly complimentary of me even to his best friend and to others in his circle. As a result, I remember feeling secure in that initial stage of our relationship.

In the second stage a predator **isolates** the victim. The predator works hard to detach you from any outside influence that could interfere with their ability to control and manipulate you. If a predator can remove you from your external support systems—family, friends, job, financial streams, etc. —they will be in position to dictate and compel your every action. In addition, a predator aims to isolate you by maligning the character of family or friends. By controlling who you talk to, predators limit the chance of an outside threat to the victim mindset they cultivate within you.

Predators seek to define who you are and what you will become. They dictate your emotions and cause mental instability. In this stage, you are more likely to believe every word they say, even if deep down you disagree or know it is not true. A predator seeks to remake you into the image they want. Therefore, they dictate areas such as your clothes, makeup, and hair along with your behavior and demeanor. If you dare protest, the onslaught is vicious and fierce. Moreover, the backlash is pervasive and unpredictable, which makes it difficult to plan an escape.

In my case, Myles hammered me to leave my job and pursue full-time, real estate investment. I already owned a triplex. My daughter and I lived for free because the back two units covered the note. I loved real estate. I could talk shop about real estate non-stop. I dreamed of being an entrepreneur, but I would never jeopardize the livelihood of my daughter. I refused to quit my job. But I acquiesced to the idea of a sabbatical where I worked part-time and pursued investment with him two days a week. His intent was to isolate me from the financial security of my work and the friends I had there.

The third stage is to **invent** the rules on a whim. This is done by changing the response and the rules as it suits them. There is no level playing ground, and you cannot gain a footing because the rules change. What was acceptable one day is suddenly not acceptable the next day. Every time I gathered my clothes in the middle of the night and fled to a girlfriend's house or to a suite in a hotel, he persistently sought me out. Once he tracked me down, he would not leave me alone. Numerous calls followed. Sometimes he would seek to woo me back with promises, behavior changes and sweet honey-coated words. At other times, he would threaten and use bitter words that sting and burn like vinegar. Regardless of the tactic, once I returned there was always the obligatory get together. I call it the "fornicate and fight syndrome." Under it all, the threat remained sinister and growing in strength.

The fourth stage is to **introduce** the threat of violence and see how the victim handles it. This is a manipulative tactic used to keep and maintain complete control as well as to "groom" the victim to accept aggressive behavior. The predator plants a seed—the potential—of the harm he could inflict should you not comply with their every demand and meet their every need. The abuser may threaten or push and shove the victim. The victim often reacts by working harder to keep the abuser calm. During this phase, the victim may believe she can prevent a violent incident, but she is walking on eggshells. Her efforts typically fail.

Myles "confided" in me about how his ex-girlfriend hurt him by lying to him habitually. Her lies led to an altercation, and he actually kicked her. He also told me about how he took anger management classes as a result. He blamed her for the stain on his record, using all his powers of persuasion to "show" me that **he** was the one wronged by her continual lies in order to gain my sympathy and allegiance. The instant that I learned he physically accosted another girlfriend should have set off an alarm. For some reason I did not think it would happen to me.

If the predator escalates to violence, they may hit, beat, sexually or verbally abuse, or use weapons against their partner. Women's lives are most often in danger. After violence there is the "honeymoon" phase. The predator apologizes to the victim and promises he will not harm her again. He may also blame his actions on her behavior. Often, the victim accepts the abuser's apologies and forgives his behavior. The cycle repeats until the victim escapes, intervention occurs, or the worst— irreparable injury or death.

Each time the cycle of violence is repeated, it escalates. If you are involved with an intimate partner who is verbally abusive, do not dismiss the possibility of crossing the line to physical abuse. The likelihood of verbal and emotional abuse leading to physical abuse is extremely high. I can attest to this, for it happened to me.

If you are in a relationship with an abusive, intimate partner, it is time to wake up. Open your eyes! You are in danger! When you add deep, emotional feelings to a premarital partnership with a predator, it is a recipe for disaster.

I had to reprogram my mind to see truth for change to happen. In order to break free, the stronghold of deception has to be penetrated.

Personally, I thank God for the sound and godly support that helped me along that journey, particularly Dr. Kenneth C. Ulmer and Faithful Central Bible Church ministry, Al and

Hattie Holingsworth, AlHatti's Christian resort, the BOSS (Building on Spiritual Success) program, and Dr. Diane Gardner's Beautiful Women of God seminars. The ministry of these leaders laid a foundation for me to break free from predatory, premarital partnerships. They built the foundation to my new mindset, and enabled me to take a stand and find freedom. This type of support is critical for each woman endeavoring to escape the clutches of the abuse they are under and the ties that have them deceived.

Chapter Six

Intimate Partner Violence
and The Rule of Thumb

The ideology that men can exert physical dominance over women to gain submission dates back to ancient times. In 753 B.C., during the reign of Romulus in Rome, wife beating was accepted and condoned under the Laws of Chastisement. Under these laws, the husband had absolute rights to physically discipline his wife. These laws permitted the husband to beat his wife with a rod or switch as long as its circumference is no greater than the girth of the base of the man's right thumb, hence "The Rule of Thumb."

We have laws preventing this type of behavior, yet it ensues today.

Ten years after I gained the victory over predatory partners, I was amazed to discover there was a whole field of expertise on interpersonal conflict. I am passionate about leveling the playing field for victims of abuse. That passion led me to pursue graduate level studies in negotiation and conflict resolution. In my research on interpersonal conflict,

I was formally introduced to the term which described what I lived and endured daily by the U.S. Department of Health and Human Services. The name for the form of abuse I experienced is Intimate Partner Violence (IPV). Intimate Partner Violence includes victimization by current and former spouses or dating partners. In my research, there are many heartbreaking stories that carry their own warning and "expertise" in how pervasive this problem is. Here is what I learned. I believe it is vital to your survival.

The Center for Disease Control and Prevention (CDC) is responsible 24/7 to protect America from health, safety, and security threats, both foreign and in the U.S. Every sixty seconds, twenty-four people are victims of violence from an intimate partner in the U.S. (www.thehotline.org). CNN reported in May of 2019, the United Nations stated that: "Thirty-five % of women worldwide have experienced violence from an intimate partner "(www.-m.cnn.com). In their presentation, Breaking the Silence—Public Health's Role in Intimate Partner Violence Prevention, intimate partner violence is listed as affecting approximately twelve million women per year. Anything that affects twelve million people is an epidemic. Awareness and education are key components, especially for women, to avoid being one of those statistics.

You may wonder precisely what intimate partner violence is. Posted on the Office on Women's Health's website (https://www.womenshealth.gov/relationships-and-safety/domestic-violence), intimate partner violence (IPV) "includes physical, sexual, or emotional abuse, as well as sexual coercion and stalking by a current or former intimate partner. "[i] It goes on to state: "An intimate partner is a person with whom you have or had a close personal or sexual relationship. Intimate partner violence affects millions of women each year in the United States. "[ii]

How does intimate partner violence happen? Intimate partners have both a public and a private face. Abuse occurs in the relationship when the public and private faces are distinctly different. It is what happens behind closed doors when there is no audience and where the social conventions of disapproval are absent. More specifically, IPV is what happens when close, interpersonal interactions between men and women moves beyond constructive communication to a crisis, and someone is deliberately hurt.

I interviewed a colleague as research for this book. He is a police lieutenant. I cannot reveal his name for privacy and safety reasons. However, he gave me permission to print this accurate account of a domestic violence case he encountered while on patrol. Here are the disturbing facts he shared:

"I have a story for you," he said.

"What?" I asked intently.

He shared, "I was on duty when I received a call to respond to a domestic violence report. I had responded to calls at this house before. The husband verbally abused the wife. I arrived at the scene. The wife had a black eye but no other serious injuries.

"This time, the wife told me, 'I am moving out!' I asked, 'Do you have a safe place to go?' She replied, 'Yeah. I am going with my mom.'

"I stayed there to protect her while she gathered her belongings and verified, she left safely. I finished my shift and left duty. It was a Friday.

"On Monday, I started my shift, and a dispatch call came through. A husband reported, 'I think I killed my wife.'

"When I heard the address, I told dispatch I was on my way. I arrived at the scene. It was the same house where I helped the wife move [from] on Friday.

"There she was, lifeless on the couch. The husband choked her to death."

I gasped! My heart instantly broke for the loss of the life of a woman I did not know but whose story I could certainly relate to.

He continued, "The husband lured her back to the house by telling her she left a few things, and it would be okay to come back and get them. When she arrived, he killed her."

He added, "We respond to domestic violence calls at least once a day and several times a week. Most women don't leave abusive relationships because they don't have a place to go, they don't have money to go, or they are ashamed. They are embarrassed and they feel stupid."

I asked if the calls occurred less often since there were more organizations around to help and more information available about violence against women. I was curious if my story was isolated, or if there was a legitimate need to tell what I went through in order to provide help and hope for other women like me.

He responded, "Everyone is talking about #MeToo [1]. Don't get me wrong, dealing with sexual harassment is important. But it is more dangerous for women to go home at night than it is to be on the street. Domestic violence occurs all the time, and it is not getting any better. No one really talks about it. You were fortunate you got out. It's all psychological control. Most women don't get out. I'd be very interested in reading your book when it comes out."

---

[1] A social movement against sexual harassment and sexual assault.

Chapter Seven

Health and Intimate Partner Violence

IPV is a significant public health issue that has considerable societal costs. Approximately forty-one percent of female IPV survivors and fourteen percent of male IPV survivors experience some form of physical injury or violence. IPV can also extend beyond physical injury and result in death. Data from U.S. crime reports suggest that sixteen percent (about 1 in 6) of murder victims are killed by an intimate partner, and that over forty percent of female homicide victims in the U.S. are killed by an intimate partner.

There are also other negative health outcomes. IPV, can cause a range of cardiovascular, gastrointestinal, reproductive, musculoskeletal, and nervous system conditions, many of which are chronic in nature. Survivors experience mental health problems such as depression and posttraumatic stress disorder (PTSD), as well as breast, uterine, and cervical cancer. Abusive words manifest themselves in the body.

The story below and my own informal experience suggest that there is a correlation between abuse and health.

"She Stayed too Long."

I attended a women's retreat in Inglewood, CA under Dr. Kenneth C. Ulmer. Dr. Beverly "Bam" Crawford was the guest speaker. She shared a story about her friend in the ministry. Dr. Crawford described her as a beautiful vibrant woman, changing lives for Christ. She recounted her joy whenever they ran into each other at re-occurring conferences. One year she did not see her friend at the conference or any ministry events. Time passed and their paths did not cross. One day she ran into her friend again. Her excitement and joy were quickly replaced with concern because her friend was in a wheelchair and frail. At the next conference, upon learning that her friend was not in attendance, Dr. Crawford inquired about her whereabouts. When she learned that her friend died of a brain tumor, she was deeply troubled. She cried for her friend. And cried out to the Lord asking "Why? If ever there was a woman more on fire for God it was her!"

I recall three things I learned from that testimony that changed my life forever. The first thing I learned was a tangible relationship with the Lord is real. Dr. Crawford had a tangible relationship with the Lord that enabled her to inquire of Him, "Why?" It was clear that she knew the Lord's ways. I was surprised to hear her say, "You know He does not have to answer (the inquiry)." By grace, He did respond to her plea. The second life changing thing I learned about this testimony was the truth from the response God gave her. I will never forget the answer, "She stayed (in the abusive marriage) too long." The answer meant that even in a marriage, God gave her the grace to leave, but she did not act on it immediately and her life was the cost. That is a deep truth that increased my spiritual maturity on the spot. The third truth that changed my life was the result of verbal abuse. Abuse manifests itself in the body. This testimony troubled me. I did not know you could die from verbal abuse.

I thought about my own physical health. I remembered my OBGYN telling me that I had a 50/50 chance of bringing my daughter into this world because the fibroid tumors were growing, feeding on estrogen, and developing its own blood supply. As soon as I heard those words, I set my will, determined that the fibroids would not abort her birth and that I would deliver her into the world. I thought also of other women I knew who had uterine fibroid tumors. Each one suffered some form of abuse in their childhood or adult lives. I did not like the correlation of abuse to tumor formation.

The testimony of Dr. Crawford, as well as the police officer's observations and experiences on the job, show most women don't escape these abusive relationships. Here was firsthand evidence of the twelve million victim statistics reported by the CDC. More needs to be done to empower women and give them the tools to get out of abusive relationships.

Lives are depending on it.

Tacit Tactics

Intimate partner violence may present in a variety of ways, depending on the relationship and circumstances. I will share with you some personal stories that demonstrate the various tactics predators use to dominate their victims.

Withholding Love

The type of predator I encountered is not the kind that utters the words "I love you" and tricks you into bondage. No, this kind of predator operates by withholding the thing you desire most—genuine love. They dangle a "promise" of that love in order to hold their victim captive and under their control. Anyone who "just wants to be loved" and suffers from insecurities in any way about being lovable, desirable, and worthy is vulnerable to this type of predator.

A predator begins courting you with compliments and talks of the kind of woman they want to marry. Unknowingly, you begin to check off the list of traits they list as desirous. The first time you change your behavior or appearance to appease a predator is the first step toward bondage. Reinforcing that control over your decisions, a predator praises every adjustment you make. As the relationship progresses, you finally achieve all of the things on their list. You are ready to receive the prize of love and acceptance and open up your heart fully to the man you have worked so hard to be worthy of.

But that prize never comes. The predator announces that you are not good enough, citing some flaw or deficit and withholds those precious three words you have been dying to hear. They may even go so far as to say there is someone else and/or just break off the relationship entirely. Whatever the case may be, the message is clear you are not good enough to be loved.

You are stunned with disbelief. After all you have done for him, he had the audacity to _____ (fill in the blank). You gave your life to him literally, making yourself over and constructing your life to suit him and his demands and pleasure. Yet he cannot even give you _____ (fill in the blank). Where is the "I love you." the ring, and the proposal? Where is the prince? You feel absolutely and one-hundred percent betrayed!

This type of predator is extremely smart. They know that withholding what you really want will only make you work harder to achieve the goal. They play on your insecurities in order to get what **they** want. The harder you work, the further down the rabbit hole you go, until you lose sight of who **you** are.

Branding

Predators always leave their mark to identify you as their property. Humans who are sold and trafficked are often branded with tattoos and, more recently, barcodes. In the relationship setting, a predator may suggest they have always wanted a woman with a tattoo with a certain symbol, or their name, or their initials. If the woman refuses to accept the brand, they will have to be prepared for the verbal onslaught of accusations, questioning her true love for him. "If you really loved me, you would show it" is a common argument to persuade you bend to his wishes.

Then, there is branding that is expressed through other ways and means other than body art called marking. For example, marking can occur through the form of an expensive gift that he expects you to use or wear. I would also caution you about another type of branding that occurs—physical abuse. The bruising from his fists, open, hand, or foot also signifies that you are his to do with as he pleases. The point is: Branding is whatever signifies his *ownership* of you.

The predator I fell captive to definitely liked to brand to show the world I was his. For him, it was a progressive branding in order to establish ownership. He showered me with expensive gifts and clothing and insisted that I wear them. He eventually used physical violence against my person to mark his territory.

I did avoid being tattooed. The response I gave for not tattooing his initials or name on my body was simply this: "If you want me to bear your name privately, then you will need to marry me, so I can bear it publicly as well." Since marriage is a covenant that this type of predator will generally not enter into, then this request was an effective argument on my part.

Gaining Access

Predators always insist on access. Access is essential for control. In my case, it was demanding access to my friends, my job, my phone, and my home. Gaining control over who I saw, what I did, where I went, my conversations, and my safe spaces. All this led to his ability to monitor outside influences as well as manipulate me and the situation for his benefit.

For instance, if my phone rang, he always made it a point to announce his presence. Moreover, his presence would overshadow the conversation, affecting what I could and could not say. Then, I was rarely "allowed" out of his sight except for work or to use the bathroom. He needed to know where I was and what I was doing at all times. Some of the ugliest battles we ever fought were over a key to my place. He wanted the right to come and go as he pleased, without question or permission.

Of course, access rights are never reciprocated. I would suggest that in the majority of cases, if not all of them, you are never invited over to his house or introduced to his friends or given a key. If you dare pick up his phone to answer it, there is a heavy price to pay. Whatever "concessions" given in the way of access have an ulterior motive or safeguard in place that still allows him to keep control of the situation (e. g. video surveillance in his home when he's not there, friends of his that report back to him, etc.).

Access through Sleep Deprivation: I saw a documentary once about the effects of sleep deprivation on drivers. The documentary showed drivers operating a vehicle on a test course after progressive levels of sleep deprivation. A handful of sleep produced disastrous results behind the wheel. Drivers did not swerve to avoid simulated obstacles or pedestrians. They simply ran over them. Their judgment, reason, and focus were all compromised due to lack of sleep.

Sleep deprivation is often used as a form of torture by an abuser in an attempt to "break" the mind of their victim. They do this to gain *access* to the information they have and/or maintain the upper hand due to their target's compromised mental state. Myles used sleep deprivation as a weapon. I would be up almost all night, and occasionally all night, purposely engaged in some sort of all-encompassing behavior, verbal confrontations, physical altercations, or sexual relations. As a result, my ability to focus in the daytime was affected, and my ability to reason clearly diminished. This was all done in an attempt to break down my resistance so that I gave him whatever he wanted and to keep me confused and broken.

Abuse assaults you on multiple levels and in many forms, preying on your emotions and manipulating your behavior. Every time you try to get out from under it, emotional ties and crippling fear ensnare you. Each time you find yourself back in the same situation again, hope dims until you cannot feel anymore. You become numb and unresponsive.

Rescuer

I tend to see the good in people despite their apparent shortcomings. I was also a classic rescuer. My adoptive mom called it the "Florence Nightingale Syndrome." Back then, I was always helping someone out without question instead of exercising wisdom and discernment. I forgot to allow the Lord to dictate when a situation needed my help and when it did not.

The Parable of the Wise and Foolish Virgins illustrates the importance of using wisdom even when others ask you for help. Matthew 25:1-13 reads:

"Then the kingdom of heaven shall be likened to ten virgins who took their lamps and went out to meet the bridegroom. Now five of them were wise, and five were foolish. Those who were foolish took their lamps and took no oil with them, but the wise took oil in their vessels with their lamps. But while the bridegroom was delayed, they all slumbered and slept. And at midnight a cry was heard: 'Behold, the bridegroom is coming; go out to meet him!' Then all those virgins arose and trimmed their lamps. And the foolish said to the wise, 'Give us some of your oil, for our lamps are going out.' But the wise answered, saying, 'No, lest there should not be enough for us and you; but go rather to those who sell, and buy for yourselves.' And while they went to buy, the bridegroom came, and those who were ready went in with him to the wedding; and the door was shut. Afterward the other virgins came also, saying, 'Lord, Lord, open to us!' But he answered and said, 'Assuredly, I say to you, I do not know you. Watch therefore, for you know neither the day nor the hour in which the Son of Man is coming."

In this passage, the wise virgins judged the situation correctly when asked for help. Had they shared their supply of oil, they and the young women they helped would have both lost out with their lamps running out of oil (verse 9). Not every cry for help or need should be personally handled by you. Based on what we learn in this Scripture, helping someone else outside of wisdom, discernment, and God's will can actually land you in trouble like it did for me.

My unrestrained rescuer mentality caused me to fall for the deception of a predator. I sympathized with him and his side of the story. Glossing over his faults, I justified his actions. Without the discernment and wisdom from the Lord, I fell prey to his manipulation and lies, becoming emotionally entangled. I was living under the despair and despondency of an abusive relationship. I tried to escape a number of times. Nevertheless, I was trapped and vulnerable to continued exploitation.

Patterns

Being in this battle is *not* your fault. More often than not, the abuser chose you. It began with a pursuit, followed by a strategic pattern—and you were an unwitting participant. The quest to draw you into this situation starts with what the abusive suitor did to get your attention.

There is nothing inherently wrong with a suitor making efforts to woo a lady. The principle that must be remembered is this: There is no difference between a predator and a prince. They *both* treat you like a queen. It all depends on the motives of the heart.

Lincoln was an island unto himself, not accountable to anyone. Although he attended church regularly, he was also a self-proclaimed loner. I could not see, nor did I take the time to discover, how he interacted with people and if he could form stable relationships—a red flag. The intensity of his pursuit had red flags attached to it as well.

Lincoln persisted until he got what he wanted, using every technique available. He finally caught me in a question to which I had no answer, and being blind to his tactics, partly because I had no deeper standards other than surface ones, I yielded. His pattern was persistence to the point of capture. Gifted at talking, he was a recruiter, engaging in conversations with me, acquiring information for his own personal use. Then, using his powers of persuasion, he took that information to manipulate and get his way. It is the very pattern of a predator.

It is critical to recognize predatory behavior patterns. Observe potential suitors in a group setting and see how they behave. What are his typical reactions? How does he talk to and/or treat people? Also, Proverbs 11:14 offers a strategy for dating, *"… in the multitude of counselors, there is safety."* Pay attention if your friends and family do not like someone. Are they picking up on things you are not? Get feedback from trusted, godly sources, like a pastor, mentor, or close friend. All can provide counsel that help you sort out possible patterns in a potential suitor. The point is, you must be wise to the pursuit and the pattern and educate yourself on behavior and negotiation skills. In order to discover the motives of a suitor's heart, you need to be able to identify the ways and means used by abusers to lure in their prey.

An older woman told me that men are designed to work, and some men use this inherent drive to work *at you*. Another woman told me that her mom told her everything men would say to get their way in order to help her recognize it when she heard it.

Another key to the pursuit is understanding a predator's type. I discovered Lincoln was cheating on me. When I met the woman, he was cheating on me with. It was then that I realized that I was his type: smart, educated, a career woman, and self-reliant. This other woman was like me, intelligent, educated, career oriented, and self-sufficient. Again, having a type is not wrong, but the heart motives behind why a suitor chases after a certain type is a determining factor in whether or not he is a prince or a predator.

The First Predator

Let's examine the words of the first and most famous conversation in the Bible. The conversation between Eve and the first predator satan.

> *Now the serpent was more cunning than any beast of the field which the Lord God had made. And he said to the woman, "Has God indeed said, 'You shall not eat of every tree of the garden'?"*

> *And the woman said to the serpent, "We may eat the fruit of the trees of the garden; but of the fruit of the tree which is in the midst of the garden, God has said, 'You shall not eat it, nor shall you touch it, lest you die.'"*

> *Then the serpent said to the woman, "You will not surely die. For God knows that in the day you eat of it your eyes will be opened, and you will be like God, knowing good and evil."*

Legal entry into this world must come through a woman. The enemy understood that there was no other way to access humanity without first manipulating. He also knew the role words and emotions played in a woman, so he used her as his access point.

Therefore, your role as a woman in society is critical. Your role is so important on earth that you were specifically and intentionally targeted from the time of creation. Why? Because you are the means of access—the portal. Through deceiving you, the enemy now has the entry or access point controlled by his "standards" and narrative. To combat his attack, we must adopt the strategy of discernment.

Solving Word Problems

Solving word problems is the toughest part of physics. The key to solving the problem is deciphering the meaning of the words. One of the first lessons I learned was to examine the words said about me and the words I said about myself. I did not realize how much I embraced (accepted what was said as true) words other people said about me without genuinely examining what was said.

Here is an example. When I was a teen, a family member said, "You have book sense but no street sense." The comment referred to my life experience or exposure. There were certain experiences I simply had no knowledge of. As I grew older, whenever I made a mistake in judgment, I would shrug it off and cover my embarrassment by repeating the words, "I have no street sense."

Here is the strategy I learned to deal with words. First, ask, "Are they true?" For example, I was only a child. I was not supposed to have "street sense" because I did not spend my time in the streets. I was on the porch with my grandmother, doing chores, in school, or curled up with a book. Second, the statement implies something is wrong if you do not have both. The words were meant as an explanation for my naivety. The words also carried a judgment against me and my "lack of knowledge" as unacceptable. What happens if I accept them? If I received the statement as true, then I limit my future and my ability. I may become defensive and retort, "I **do** have street sense!" Or the words may plant a seed of curiosity and may lead to exploring in places I did not belong. I may ponder, *"I wonder what she means by street sense? I am going to get some!"* Neither response is good. Here is the Word of God you can use to judge spoken words: John 10:10, *"The devil comes to kill, steal and destroy but I have come that thou may have life and more abundantly."* To determine the nature of words, ask yourself, "Do the words bring life?" Or are the words intended "to steal, kill and destroy." The words we hear and use on a daily basis have to be vigorously dissected like a biology project before you accept them as truth.

Here is a simple exercise. 1. Write down all the negative words people say or have said about you. 2. Write down the words you say about yourself. For each statement, ask yourself if the words are meant to help or harm. Helpful words align with the truth of God's Word and are intended to give life. Harmful words are accusatory, and they intend to steal, kill, and destroy.

Spewing Venom

We have talked about the pursuit. Now, let's talk about the pattern in relation to the battle. First, what is the pattern? Well, it starts with attacks targeting your ears.

In my first relationship, while I was compliant, everything was copacetic. As soon as I disagreed with my partner, a persistent barrage of words was unleashed in order to "convince" me to comply. The more I resisted, the more aggressive he became, until my defenses were too weak to withstand the onslaught.

I call attacks like these "spewing venom" because the words were literally poisoned. Spewing venom is an onslaught of negative words and demeaning comments designed to do one thing—go for the jugular vein and sever any attempt at resistance. The attack is designed to stun, create pain, and then quickly, repeatedly, and loudly hurl verbal insults in order to incapacitate you so you cannot defend yourself.

An abuser's verbal attacks have a pattern. The attacks happen behind closed doors or in confined spaces, although it can occur in other ways other ways and means, such as over the phone. The attacker *controls you with fear*. That fear is reinforced through their words and accusations.

Denying any accusations does not stop the attack. Pleading with them to leave or to cease does not prevent the attack.

Fleeing in the middle of the night does not stop the attack. The first thing you will have to deal with in an abusive relationship is fear.

What is the fear that is being used to control or manipulate you? For me, the fear was being alone and not married. In my desperate desire to be married, I tried my best to make my relationships work because I wanted to get to a proposal. What is your fear? Is it in being single and alone? Is it abandonment? Is it being left to take care of the kids all by yourself? Whatever the root of your fear, why you are being held captive to it has to be dealt with in order to take steps toward freedom.

Where War Is Waged

Abuse is primarily a mental and emotional battle. My mind and emotions were engaged full-time in dealing with abuse. Because of the uncertainty I faced, the "on edge" feeling I lived with, the constant drama, and the reactionary state of my mind and emotions, I never could stop to think about or truly evaluate what was going on. The "not being able to stop and pause" is by design. It is a power and control tactic of your abuser. You cannot be strategic if you do not have time to plan and think.

The battle is waged on all fronts. It has a physical component, referring to the actual steps you take to gain your freedom. The mind is where you process what you are going through, how you view yourself, and how you address faulty mindsets and patterns that have hindered you. For example, I had to overcome self-esteem issues as well as learn to deal properly with conflict, anger, and trust. Finally, wisdom is needed to develop strategies and plans to move forward. Often, intervention or outside help is required to help you move past this tactic.

Chapter Nine

Masquerade

The years I dated Myles were filled with drama—bullying, invasion of privacy, manipulation, sleep deprivation, name-calling, and later on physical violence. In fact, drama was a regular item on the menu at my house. Plus, I was always compared to other women he dated previously and deemed unworthy by him on a daily basis. Nothing I did ever pleased him.

As a result, I became an expert at wearing a mask. My public self was a success, but my private self was a mess. Yet, despite my efforts to keep my private hell private, I still could not hide the whole truth of what I was going through, for none of my friends approved of my involvement with him.

Getting to the core of the matter is what I call "drilling down to the lowest common denominator." Drilling down means asking yourself "Why?" until you get to the core and identify root reasons that led to your belief system and kept you in bondage. I did this process with regard to Myles. Why do I stay? I stay because I love him. Why do you love him? I love him because he revered me when we met. He put me on a pedestal and supported all of my accomplishments. We made a great team. And so on.

Those questions finally led to my discovery of the justification—the lie—I was telling myself. "We are just having communication issues." I rationalized what was going on and did not see it for what it really was—abuse. I realized that I was in love with his potential, not his actual. I was caught in the trap of waiting for his actual to catch up with his potential. Unfortunately, potential is tied to character, the critical sixth "C" that is necessary for every prince to possess, something Myles did not have.

As I continued to drill down to the core of the issue, it dawned on me one day that his potential *was* his actual. Let's look back to the five wise virgins in the parable. They were sympathetic, and recognized the problem. And they assisted but not in the way they were asked. They provided aid, wise advice, and set boundaries, in a way that was helpful *but did not endanger their own standing*. When I was blinded to the fact that Myles's potential could never reach prince status without a transformation of character, I put myself in danger, unknowingly subjecting myself to abuse.

Why is it important to drill down to the lowest common denominator? If you can give a name to your opponent, you can fight it. Often, your opponent is simply a lack of knowledge

—knowledge of: who you are, your value, and your rights. It also includes the truth about how *any* woman *should* be treated, what constitutes IPV and abuse, what are the characteristics of a predator, and so on. Once you understand the root of the matter and what needs to change, then you can take steps and take a stand.

The next question is: Who has the knowledge on how to get out of these situations? For me, I could not find anyone. Everyone just *said* to me, "I wouldn't put up with that! You need to leave him!" While that was certainly true, no one told me **how** to get out.

Unfortunately, I lost friendships because I lingered in the relationship. Back then, I wish I had known someone who was willing to be transparent about what they had gone through and share how they got free. I could have used a testimony from someone who had walked the path before me. Then I could see that I was not alone and find a firm foundation to stand on in order to make changes. It is critical to share one's story regarding IPV, as hard as it is, to help other women in similar situations figure out their "how."

The one person who did tell me Myles was a predator was a victim of abuse herself (by her dad). She recognized it and understood. She offered me the world's way of getting out—cuss him out and lock the door. The world's solution won several battles for me, but it did not win the war. Myles always came back with a vengeance. I needed to find another way.

Myles was a church-going brother. He never missed a day of reading the Word and going to church. My grandmother put it best: "He may be in church, but the church is not in him." Words of wisdom to heed spoken by an octogenarian.

The truth imparted to me through my reoccurring dream or nightmare literally scared me. I felt this truth take hold with intensity. Without the tongue, you are mute, unable to speak. Your voice is unique—like a signature or a thumbprint. In my reoccurring dream, I fought to regain the control of my tongue, so I could breathe, live, and have a voice. The feelings of fear after each nightmare served as my wake-up alarm, prompting me to eventually take action. The dream continued to plague me until my relationship with Myles stopped.

Myles was not my true opponent. I had to face the fear of being alone. I also had to face the fear of taking care of myself after relying so heavily on him in many areas. If you are financially dependent on him or have co-mingled your finances, this fear is definitely heightened. Then there's the fear of what to say when others ask you "How is so and so doing?" Remember, fear is a liar. It will keep you bound to the problem and blind to the solution.

Most of us spend too much time fighting with our abuser or defending ourselves from their onslaught. We are caught up in an endless cycle that does not allow us to drill down to the lowest common denominator. When I began to *disengage* in order to examine the scenario, I could better face my fears and see the solution. I encourage you to spend less time engaging and more time strategizing and partnering with the Lord.

IPV and other abuse can be complicated, so it is crucial that you remember Ephesians 6:12: *"... we do not wrestle against flesh and blood, but against principalities, against powers, against the rulers of the darkness of this age, against spiritual hosts of wickedness in the heavenly places."*

I want you to be like the sons of Issachar in 1 Chronicles 12:32 *"who had understanding of the times, to know what Israel ought to do."* Wisdom is needed.

Wisdom taught me my dream was a mirror. It was a reflection in the spirit of what was happening in the natural realm of my life. For anyone caught in the web of IPV/abuse, the dream holds great significance. Your tongue symbolizes your voice. Without your tongue, you cannot speak. The enemy's contract on your life is *"to steal, and to kill, and to destroy"* as stated in John 10:10. You must reclaim your voice. To do that, you must also discover your value and worth— who you are.

Chapter Ten

Hear No Evil

Women are influenced by what they hear. Men are influenced by what they see. Think back to the last argument you had. I can guarantee that afterwards, you mulled over the words that were said. This is a critical point. Words have power to influence and are therefore access points. Words are access points because we make decisions based on emotions that arise from words. Replaying conversations in our mind reinforces emotions. When emotions are fully grown, they produce action. The equation is: Words + Emotions = Action.

The enemy influences women by what they hear. To understand the root of violence against women, we need information about its origin. Here is the key from Genesis 3:15, *"I will put enmity between you and the woman and between your seed and her seed."* The enemy, satan[2] is an ancient and treacherous foe.

---

[2] Lowercase is intentional

The enemy is a foe of women because legal entry into the earth has to come through a woman. Science may have advanced to the point where an egg can be combined with spermatozoa and grow to a certain point. But in order to give life, to create thinking, walking, talking, breathing human life, the fertilized egg has to be implanted into a female. A female is essential to the preservation of humanity.

The manner in which the enemy undermines women is shrewd. In the Bible there are only two recorded conversations between a human and satan. The enemy speaks to Jesus in the desert, tempting him after fasting. The enemy speaks to Eve in Genesis 3:1 The enemy asks, "Has God indeed said, You shall not eat from every tree in the garden?"

The enemy plants the seed of doubt so subtly. Doubt and truth cannot coexist. One will dominate the other. Doubt is like cracking the door, taking a peek to see what is inside. The door of femininity is to be shut until its appointed time. Cracking the door allows the enemy to gain a foothold and continue to pry open places that should be shut. When women compromise their position of strength and crack the door, all hell literally comes in. In the Song of Solomon 8:9 there is a clue about our position as women: *"If she is a wall, we will build upon her, a battlement of silver; And if she is a door, we will enclose her with boards of cedar."* The verse refers to a young woman before she reaches maturity. The medical term for this stage of human development is preadolescent. The medical definition of preadolescence according to Merriam Webster is "the period of human development just preceding adolescence specifically: the period between the approximate ages of nine and twelve."

The mental maturity of the girl is formed in preadolescence. A young girl whose self-esteem is intact knows her value and self-worth and assumes a position of strength. She is referred to as a wall upon which you can build a battlement of silver. The battlement is the highest place of protection built on a solid wall with openings to shoot weapons and defeat the enemy. Silver is a precious metal used in ancient civilizations as a commodity as it is today. It is valuable, shiny, resists corrosion, and conducts heat.

Wow! The enemy is always trying to breach the wall and gain access to the battlement. A girl who does not know her purpose and her position of strength is a door. She is open and susceptible to breach. As women, we wear many hats: leader, mother, wife, teacher, and friend. As leaders, if we are doors that can be manipulated, those who we train are susceptible to deception. As mothers if we are doors, the enemy can destroy our entire family line. Husbands, children, and households are in jeopardy. If we are not in place as the nurturer, the enemy attacks our self-esteem. If we are not in our place as friends, gossip will enter in and destroy the lives of those we cherish. If chaos is running rampant in your home, your relationships, your work life, check to see if your door is open. If it is, give the enemy an eviction notice and close your door.

The cedar girds the door in the verse. Cedar is a highly sought-after wood known for its pleasant smell, lack of rot, and resistance to bugs. We are created in God's image according to Genesis. Anatomically and emotionally speaking, we are designed to receive and produce good things. There is power in what we produce. The enemy has an issue with this.

He gained legal entry into this world through the woman. How? With *words*. The enemy used words to manipulate the woman's emotions, generating a response. When that response was subsequently confirmed by the man, the trap set by the enemy was full grown.

How shrewd and strategic was that conversation with Eve in the Garden of Eden! That crucial conversation with Eve used words to create doubt. The enemy twisted the meaning of God's instructions, causing her to question what God had said.

She was secure until she believed the words satan told her.

Part Two

Break Free

Understanding Truth

In my journey, I discovered six key truths that I want to share with you. These truths are foundational. Building your house of freedom on a solid foundation will ensure it weathers the storm. Here is an illustration: I was looking to purchase a home. I saw some new homes under construction in my neighborhood and decided to tour a model. It was beautiful! I decided to buy it, and I was excited! The sales agent gave me the purchase and sale agreement that was equivalent to a mini-book to read and sign. At the back of the purchase and sale agreement, there was a disclosure section. The disclosure section revealed that the foundation of the home showed cracks when it was inspected and that the issue was remedied with epoxy. After reading the disclosure, I exclaimed, "Epoxy! Isn't that glue?" If the foundation is corrupt, the home will shift. Cracks will appear along the walls, and the structural integrity is compromised. I offer these foundational truths so that your home is solid and to encourage you to ignite your voice.

Truth #1 - It is about you.

The most remarkable mental shift for me occurred when I saw my life from God's point of view. I no longer maintained a mental list of all the wrongs I endured. Instead, I sought to discover how God thought of me and to build up my self-esteem in Him. Mental conversations about what the predator I dated said or did to me ceased.

Slowly, painfully I acknowledged the truth—No one could do anything to me I did not subconsciously allow. Now, this truth was a *harsh* reality check for me. Am I saying abuse is deserved? Not! **No one** deserves abuse. What I am specifically acknowledging is our level of self-esteem plays a huge role in what signals we send out. If I had possessed the confidence and satisfaction in myself that matched how God viewed me, I would not have fallen for the deception. A predator could not have exploited my insecurities. Here is a quote to underscore this truth:

"If you are not being treated with love and respect, check your price tag. Maybe you have marked yourself down. It's you who tells people what you're worth. Get off the clearance rack and get back behind the glass where they keep the valuables." – Author Unknown

In order to truly rediscover your voice, you also have to rediscover your value. As you value yourself and build your self-esteem, your voice will become stronger and more confident. In the end, it **is** all about you.

Truth #2 - You are not alone.

If you think you are alone in a struggle, think again. Consider the following statistics from the Center for Disease Control:

> *IPV is common. It affects millions of people in the U.S. each year. Data from CDC's National Intimate Partner and Sexual Violence Survey (NISVS) indicate nearly one in four (25%) of adult women and approximately one in seven (14%) of adult men report having experienced severe physical violence from an intimate partner in their lifetime.*

Statistics tell us that IPV is not an isolated problem. In fact, the numbers are staggering. There **is** hope. And you are *not* alone.

I am living proof to the fact that you are not alone. My book is your wake-up call to this fact.

Truth #3 - If you do not know the purpose of a thing you will abuse it.

Here is my truth for all who begin the hard, emotional work of self-discovery: *"If you do not know the purpose of a thing, you will abuse it[3]"*. This illustration highlights my point. Imagine a woman washing her hands at the bathroom sink. As she searches for something to dry her hands, she notices a fresh paper towel and a new crisp $100 bill on the counter. If she uses the $100 bill to dry her hands, crumple it up, and throw it in the trash, it provokes a reaction. Why? Aren't the paper towel and the $100 bill both made of paper? Yes, they are. Even though they are both made of paper, their purpose is not the same. One has value, and the other does not. You would not dream of throwing a $100 in the trash because of its value. We as women must not waste our value. Find out who you are and your purpose so that your value is established.

I did not know my purpose. I wasted years of my life, allowing others to define who I was and tell me what I would become. I was numb with emotional pain, floating with no roots, tossed back and forth from here to there. I was alone. I believed belonging to someone else was the answer to my pain.

---

[3] Original quote by Gina Marie, MA

Truth #4 - Protecting a predator is counterproductive.

Women are nurturers. In case you do not see yourself as a nurturer, note that nurturing may manifest in different ways but the core value is the same. Nurturing can manifest in the traditional motherly manner or as a strong desire to protect the ones you love. The desire to nurture or protect must not extend to predators.

It is critical that you do **not** take responsibility for a predator's actions. Under no circumstance did you deserve it, and despite what you may have been told by a predator (or others), you did not "make" them do it. What they did to you was their choice alone. Therefore, allow the penalties for their actions to take place. Do not interrupt the law of sowing and reaping according to Galatians 6:7, *"Do not be deceived, God is not mocked; for whatever a man sows, that he will also reap."* Those who cross boundaries can only discover the opportunity to learn from their bad choices when they face the consequences.

Truth #5 - All men are not predators.

It is a natural defense mechanism and coping mechanism to put all men into the foe category after suffering abuse at the hands of a man. This behavior is understandable. However, what happens when a good man tries to interact with you? If your emotions are not healed, you will snap his head off with words, or you will condemn him and be distrustful of him. You will pounce the second he does or says something that triggers hurt from the past. A huge part of healing from past wounds is learning how to interact with all people and discern their intentions.

Truth #6 - It is not too late.

I started the journey to healing in 1990. Thirty years later, I am still living free from predatory behavior. I am successful, confident, and enjoying life. I am a living testimony that you can find freedom and build a new life.

I will tell you that it takes effort and determination to learn about who you really are and value what God sees in you. It is never too late to start! Even if it starts with, "I don't deserve this," that is okay. That is a great place to begin! It shows that you believe—deep down—that you *do* have value. Pursue the truth, and you will find that the mask falls off the face of Intimate Partner Violence, and the counterfeit is revealed.

The winning strategy starts with you! I suggest you journal. A journal is not a diary. It is a record of your thoughts, feelings, facts, and activities. Journaling is an excellent way to get in touch with your thought processes and rediscover who you are. In evaluating how you think, you can ask yourself questions like: What do I value? What is truly important to me? What is my definition of a healthy relationship? Am I living true to that? What are my default reactions to conflict? Why do I act that way? What are my strengths? What are my weaknesses? What do I like? What do I detest? What am I good at? What makes me happy? Note that the signals we give outwardly are always tied to how we think about ourselves inwardly.

It is imperative that you begin the mental process of defining you to separate physically from a predator. This starts with figuring yourself out. A quote that resonates with me is, "Find out who you are and do it on purpose." -Dolly Parton.

A personality test is highly recommended. I took the temperament test based on the Greek physician Galen's theory that temperament correlates to the elements or the four humors or fluids found in the body: sanguine, phlegmatic, choleric, and melancholic. The test helps you discover how you think and work. Then, you can journal what you learn and how those personality influences your decisions.

As you keep a written record of what you learn about yourself, you can identify patterns or behaviors. Those things that are not supportive of who you truly are deep down are the things that need to change. Areas of thought and behavior that are not producing positive results in your life must be addressed.

A note of caution: If your partner is the kind who searches through your possessions, then keep your journal hidden. A digital journal on your phone with a passcode is an option. However, there is the risk that a predator will see the journal on your phone or computer and demand the code. If that happens say, "No!" You can leave the journal at work, obtain a safe deposit box, or find another such off-site and secure place that the predator does not have access to. Or you can leave it with a close friend who is not associated with the predator. This exercise is important, and you must find a way to do it discreetly.

Chapter Twelve

A Day of Reckoning

A trip to Alhatti's Christian Resort for a retreat was the capstone that broke the cycle of low self-esteem-abuse-fear in my life. Despite numerous obstacles, I was determined to attend.

As, we gathered in a circle to close with a prayer the leader looked in my direction and said, "Powerful woman of God, please close us out in prayer." I slowly turned my head to peer over my shoulder to see who he was talking about. He said, "I am talking to you, powerful woman of God." as he gazed directly at me. I was genuinely stunned and speechless at the new label. Nevertheless, I found my voice and began to pray. But the voice that I heard was different. It was confident. When I opened my eyes, I stood with my feet firmly planted and literally said to satan, "You should have **never** let me get up here."

When you are accustomed to a certain belief system about yourself, thinking anything else very difficult at first. Just like the body rejects anything foreign, so does the mind.

I do not remember the words I prayed that day. I only remember the surprise of considering for the first time in my life that I might be more than the "smart girl" label I had acquired.

On that day, the eyes and ears of my understanding were opened about the power that words had over me according to Ephesians 1:17-18, *"That the God of our Lord Jesus Christ, the Father of glory, may give to you the spirit of wisdom and revelation in the knowledge of Him, the eyes of your understanding being enlightened; that you may know what is the hope of His calling, what are the riches of the glory of His inheritance in the saints."*

All the shackles fell. I knew that I was bound but I saw a strategy on how to fight. I was still in the relationship. In fact, Myles was also at the retreat. But for the first time I knew how to escape, and I felt empowered to act. Healing can start in the midst of your trauma.

There are a number of steps or areas that need to be addressed if you are to break free of the abusive cycle. Remember that knowledge is power. Understanding things from a place of knowledge allows you to counteract those areas in your life that are operating under false premises and

built on faulty foundations. Knowledge is a tool that you can use, and when you apply knowledge, wisdom is the result. With wisdom, you can truly find freedom.

Chapter Thirteen

Finally, Free

Take these steps to help you get free:

Step 1 - Acknowledge the Battle

If you deny that the problem exists, you will not make any changes to break free. This also includes the subconscious role you play in the cycle in Truth #3.

The enemy is an ancient and treacherous foe. Because women are uniquely positioned in God's plan, enmity (hostility, opposition, conflict) now stands between you and the enemy of all God's creation, satan. He is the original predator and source of all predatory thinking. Every battle is about power and control. A predator uses words to gain control over you and to exert power.

Acknowledgment is the first step to freedom. Hint: If you instinctively hide this book because you know there will be consequences if your partner finds you reading it—you are in a battle.

Step 2 - Harness the Power of Peepholes

Take comfort in these words from the Lord: *"I will contend with him who contends with you."* (Isaiah 49:25). You cannot find total freedom without the Lord's help.

Peepholes allow you to see who is on the other side of the door. You can see if it is a friend or a foe and decide whether or not to open the door. Peepholes allow you to see what would otherwise be hidden. Since the door is an access point, you do not want to open it until you are sure of who is on the other side.

Partner with the Lord because the Holy Spirit gives discernment like a peephole, allowing you to see what is otherwise hidden and warning you of danger in advance for you to make a plan. Here is the song I wrote to the Lord when I made the covenant to partner with Him:

I am learning to trust You, Lord.
I am learning to trust You, Lord in all that I do.
I can't see what's coming,
but I know that You can,
Because You finished it Lord. Yes, You did.
It's all in Your hands.

Step 3 - Set Your Will

You may feel shame. You may be embarrassed. You may feel like you are a failure. You may feel like you are stupid. These emotions are strong and very real. Yet, none of these emotions affects your will. Your will is the strongest weapon you have.

To overcome abusive words, we have to bypass the conscious mind and go straight to the subconscious mind using Scripture. I would play Scripture on a compact disc at night while I slept until my outward self, the one I saw in the mirror, matched the one God created. In this way, I could separate my emotions and, with my new insight into who I really was in God, enact my will to believe the truth.

Step 4 - Understand That You Have a Choice.

Your own will may not be something you have seen in a while. Yet, if you acknowledge that there is a problem with how you are being treated, then you have already engaged your will. You are now actively logging the behavior as wrong. This is a huge step. You are to be congratulated! It took me years to believe I actually had a choice in how I was being treated.

Step 5 - Deal with Shame

Have you ever carried something heavy for a distance? As you walk the weight of the load begins to bear down. You may shift the object from one shoulder to another to compensate your body posture and proceed for a while, but the weight is heavier still. This is how undue shame feels. It is a weight from something in your past around your neck and shoulders causing you to move slowly, slump, and cast your vision downward. If you escaped a predator, I give you a standing ovation. Yes. Choosing a predator is a mistake. Mistakes must be put into their proper place. If you allow a mistake to take root, it grows into undue shame. My remedy? I learned to laugh at my mistakes, not to defend them. Defending them means I take ownership of the mistake. Laughing at it means that I acknowledge it for what it is, a mistake. Nothing more.

I do not attach judgment to the mistake. Remember this equation: A mistake plus judgment equals shame. The goal of shame is to lead you to despondency, a place of no hope. Hope is essential to thriving after an attack. It is a decision. An act of your will. Getting rid of shame is a simple act of your will. It can be eliminated in three steps: First, identify whatever judgment you attached to the mistake and say the exact opposite. Second, identify the mistake as a molehill. Mistakes alone are molehills. Mistakes with judgment are mountains. Third, say out loud, "I evict shame from my life!"

Step 6 - Evict the Victim and Be the Victor

The victim spirit prevents you from seeing yourself from God's point of view. I learned about the victim spirit while attending the Cleansing Stream Retreat after an eight-week class. This ministry is designed to help people identify and release baggage from the past, so they can live in freedom, walk in alignment, and learn to use their authority in Christ.

The victim spirit is designed to convince you that you are powerless to change your situation and that things will never get better. Negative self-talk plays like a broken record over and over again under the influence of this victim mindset: "No one will ever love me!" or "I will always feel sad/angry/depressed," or "I can't expect much good in life." A victim is also persuaded to believe what is wrong is right. The primary goal of this spirit is to replace your mindset with one that will ultimately defeat and undermine you in life. Eliminating the victim spirit and negative, self-destroying thoughts helps you to rebuild your self-esteem. You cannot change the mind or actions of a predator, but you can change, with the Lord's help, your perspective. It is about you and your freedom.

When this spirit is operating in your life, it draws predator spirits. Romans 8:31-39 has the antidote to the victim spirit:

"God's Everlasting Love

If God is for us, who can be against us? He who did not spare His own Son, but delivered Him up for us all, how shall He not with Him also freely give us all things? Who shall bring a charge against God's elect? It is God who justifies…Yet in all these things we are more than conquerors through Him who loved us. For I am persuaded that neither death nor life, nor angels nor principalities nor powers, nor things present nor things to come, nor height nor depth, nor any other created thing, shall be able to separate us from the love of God which is in Christ Jesus our Lord."

The victim spirit attacks the manner in which the brain processes information. Negative words are heard and not filtered properly. Apply Scripture to help you to take inventory —to examine and filter your thoughts through the lens of truth.

Step 7 - Discern Who Is Talking

As women, we must pay attention to words and who spoke them. Whose voice are you listening to? There are only three voices: yours, satan's, and the Lord's. It is imperative that you know whose words are operating in your life.

I counseled my twenty-year-old niece about a man her friend was involved with. I saw snapshots of her friend on her phone—a young girl whose face was beaten, her eyes were swollen shut, and there were cuts and bruises on her face. My heart broke at the site of her face in the picture. She was trapped in a cycle of abuse.

My niece believed that "first love" was the reason her friend stayed with her boyfriend. By first love, she meant that he was the first person she had been intimate with, and he was the first suitor to say he loved her.

Because the boyfriend said the words, "I love you" confusion set in. Why was there confusion? It occurred because what was said did not agree with what was done. His actions did not say, "I love you." In fact, they said the exact opposite. True love will always produce actions to support the words.

Like my niece's friend, we must evaluate each word and determine who is talking. Why? Words lead to thoughts. Thoughts lead to beliefs. Beliefs lead to actions. It is important to understand that *words* set work in motion. In order to inventory thoughts, we must take each thought off of the shelf and honestly assess it in accordance with John 10:10: *"The thief does not come except to steal, and to kill, and to destroy. I have come that they may have life, and that they may have it more abundantly."*

If the thought steals, kills, or destroys your peace or your self-esteem, then it is from the enemy. On the other hand, if the thought brings life and restoration, peace, love, and joy, then it is from the Lord. Thoughts from Him are designed to refresh, replenish, and restore. Think on those things!

What are words producing in your life? If you find yourself in a bruised, bullied, and battered state, the words you are listening to are not of God.

Step 8 - Identify Who You Have Been Believing

After you discern who is talking, the next step is to determine what you actually believe. This battle for freedom is fought primarily in your mind.

In the year 2000, I attended a Skillpath workshop and purchased a set of tapes on building strong self-esteem by Jack Canfield, an author, motivational speaker, corporate trainer, and entrepreneur. The simple truth I gleaned that helped my self-esteem was this: Words only hurt if you believe they are true.

Information enters the body, mind, and spirit through the senses. There are five senses: sight, hearing, smell, taste, and touch. Every day every human has to make a decision about every word they hear. Do you agree with what you hear? Or not? Do you believe the words or not? Who have you been believing: The voice of the enemy, Your own voice, or the voice of the Lord?

Step 9 - Use Truth to Trump Facts

Just because a statement is a fact, does not make it true. A fact is a word that is undisputed. Nevertheless, truth trumps facts every time. The second law of physics says that two objects cannot occupy the same space at the same time. Likewise, truth and facts cannot occupy the mind simultaneously.

Brokenness happens when we cannot release facts and come to terms with the truth of who God says we are.

Be willing to go through the process. The rewards are worth it!

Moving forward, it is wise to pay attention to words spoken about you. Keep a log if you need to. Then, replace any word identified as a lie with the truth found in God's Word. Read the Bible to know what God says about you.

Here is a matrix of how truth trumped facts from my life:

FACT	TRUTH
I was adopted at birth.	God restored me with my birth mom 42 years later.
My adopted father left when I was an infant.	God is a father to the fatherless.

The circumstances of your life do not dictate your future.

Step 10 - Practice the New You

Any new skill requires practice.

Therefore, in order to practice the new you, your belief system needs to be adjusted to allow both *words* and *actions* to be considered. And if the words and actions do not align, then discard and reject the words. They can't be permitted access to your thoughts in any way.

There has to be reconciliation. Like you reconcile the checks you write against the balance of your bank account, in the same way, your old self must be reconciled to your new self. You eliminate what is false and replace it with what is true. This reconciliation is an inner alignment, based on your true value as defined by God. It is what you will use to change the situation.

Chapter Fourteen

Stay Free

Step 1 - Housekeeping

Now that your house is clean. You have to make sure you keep clutter from re-entering. How? Deal with people in your life that say wrong words. The way to counteract any wrong (false) words coming at you is to declare what God says about you. Declaring builds faith, and you are better equipped to withstand such attacks against who you truly are.

Once you change your perspective, it is important to note that other people may not have changed theirs. Have a strategy for addressing their behavior. Realize that you cannot change someone else's behavior, you can only change yours. Without a strategy, you run the risk of reverting to old patterns. I developed a comeback for sayings that wounded me. For example, in response to the accusation "You don't listen!" I prepared a response. I said "Obey is not the same as listen. I have the right to hear, ponder, and make my own decision."

Ever notice how people sit in the same spot every time there is a meeting? We are creatures of habit. When change is introduced, it throws us off track if we are not prepared for it. When people see the new you, they may be critical. They may still call you by your old name. Embrace your new life and let them know you are no longer what they call you. State that the behavior they are referencing is a part of the past. You are new. It is important not to let the words gain a foothold. Respond with who God says you are. Shun negative titles from the past.

Step 2 - Reach, Walk, Pull

Sometimes, just finding a strategy to deal with other people is not enough. Sometimes you may have to excise some people from your life. As you mature, it is important to examine every relationship and determine whether or not the relationship is still a benefit to you. If the person is not in your corner, then it is time to build a new team.

Choosing new people to associate with is crucial to the journey. Equally yoked is often used to illustrate marriage. The term is a principle that cross applies to all aspects of life. To be effective, oxen are yoked so that they plow in unison, one is not ahead or behind the other. If you hang out with people who criticize you, they are toxic like poison. Find like-minded individuals who are headed in the same direction as you. Find those who encourage you to be greater than you ever thought you could be. You need a cheering squad who will applaud you. Members of your cheering squad may also give constructive correction. Do not confuse this with negative words because it is uncomfortable to hear.

Reaching, walking, and pulling is your posture. To Reach: you need those who praise you, inspire you, and challenge you to go the distance. Also remember to ask God for the right mentors. I am whole today because I worked with a mentor. To Walk: you need like-minded people alongside you. I surrounded myself with peers who had the same goals and dreams. To Pull: you need those who you encourage and pull forward. Maybe you have heard of each one, teach one and lead one. When you get free your testimony can help another who is struggling. A testimony changes a perspective in an instant. I found time to help those who struggled with the same things I did. Reaching ahead, walking alongside, and pulling others forward is the goal.

One of the most dangerous prideful thoughts is that no one understands what I am going through. Sharing a testimony will show someone else that she is not alone. My dream is to eradicate violence against women. I dream of a world where we are no longer victims but are victorious. Ignite your voice!

Step 3 - Boundaries! Don't Leave Home Without Them

There is a price for unrequited nice. People you interact with know you better than you know yourself. If you suffer from "the disease to please" and have trouble saying "no" like I did, invest the time to train yourself to set boundaries.

Without boundaries, either knowingly or unknowingly, you are at risk of being taken advantage of. It is not popular to think about the opportunistic aspect of human nature, but it is a fact. Retrain people how to treat you. Setting boundaries is essential to avoid intimate partner violence.

Here is an example:

I had a friend who was often in need of money, which she rarely paid back. She called one evening. Her story pulled at my heartstrings. I instinctively offered to help instead of taking time to ask basic questions like, "How do you intend to pay back the debt?" or "How do you plan to avoid this crisis in the future?" One day she told me of how someone gave her a freebie. In telling the story she said something that clicked. "I didn't ask, they offered." I had an instant epiphany! I finally understood her modus operandi. For her, sharing a crisis scenario with me was practically a guarantee for assistance. She knew my behavior patterns. I was her ace in the hole. Learning to set boundaries is not easy when you have a heart to give. But the gift of giving will be tainted if you do not know when to give and when not to give. To retrain people, I set boundaries for borrowing. I intentionally set up a savings account that was not linked to my bank account.

If anyone asked me to borrow money, I responded, "My money for lending is in a separate account that takes three days to cut a check." Or, I would ask them to write me a check that I could cash on their payday. I was stunned at the decrease in requests to borrow money when I commissioned this strategy. Using a strategy for lending accomplished two things: It eliminated those who asked for money as their first and only option to meet their financial obligations, and it eliminated those who did not have a plan to pay it back.

I share this example of setting boundaries and the danger of people pleasing because it is a key issue in intimate partner violence.

If I had used proper decorum and set a healthy boundary on what information to share when I met someone for a date, I would not have run incessantly at the mouth sharing every iota about my life and goals. Remember the word logorrhea from the movie *Akeelah and the Bee?* It means excessive talking at the mouth. Listen to learn and avoid divulging too many intimate details. A predator listens to you and mirrors what you tell them. You will not know what they truly believe.

I did not set a boundary and more importantly, I did not have a protocol for dating.

I would encourage you to establish some ground rules ahead of time about what happens after first dates. Avoid overfamiliarity and talking late into the evening. Establish boundaries about the time and length of conversations. Daily conversations are unhealthy unless you are engaged or married. Here is a boundary test that I used: If you cannot go for a week without talking to your potential partner you have crossed the boundary of overfamiliarity.

The key is accountability. If you trying to get the elusive carrot of love and acceptance, you might not consider whether you actually *like* this person or want to be involved with them. Does this person make you happy? Are you compatible with this person? Are they trying to change you? Without established rules, you will fall for anything.

Step 4 - Change Your Criteria

Make a list of core characteristics that are important to you. When you meet someone new, compare it to your list. I discovered that my original list of mate qualities was set by popular culture: career, credit, and charisma. When I took the time to undergo reconstruction, I emerged shiny and new. I was sending different signals through my posture, my manner of dress, my voice, and my body language. My mate characteristics changed to faithful, honorable, kind-hearted, and chivalrous.

If you do not have criteria established yet, I would encourage you to at least use wisdom like the eagle and test potential mates.

One of the best prayers I ever prayed was, "Lord, show me his heart." I learned to ask for wisdom in the area of dating after surviving intimate partner violence, not once, but twice. It was obvious to me that my decision maker was broken. As soon as I prayed this prayer, a red flag showed up.

The second most significant prayer I prayed during this season was, "Lord cover me. Any place that I am open (vulnerable), cover me." You can be instantly covered by asking the Lord right now to cover any broken places, places of desire and longing. Ask the Lord to cover these delicate emotions so that the door to satan is closed.

Step 5 - Forgive

Forgiveness forfeits your right to judge people for their offenses. It means choosing between being right or being free. I can look at Myles and Lincoln today with no animosity. That is because of the miracle of forgiveness. I would not have been able to embrace my wonderful husband today if I still carried emotional ties and unforgiveness for those in my past. According to Mark 11: 25, we are encouraged to forgive for our benefit:

"And whenever you stand praying, if you find that you carry something in your heart against another person, release him and forgive him so that your Father in heaven will also release you and forgive you of your faults. But if you will not release forgiveness, don't expect your Father in heaven to release you from your misdeeds."

Step 6 - Gates, Doors, and Walls

As women, we are not always aware the enemy works the same way in our lives today as he did in Eden—through access points. Our ears, eyes, reasoning and intellect, our desire for sexual intimacy and intercourse, etc., *All* are the equivalent to gates, doors, and walls. They are access points to our inner being and who we are and are called to be.

The enemy attempts to breach a gate, door, or wall to gain access to the hero camp and take over. The devices used to break through are always intriguing and ingenious. In one of my favorite movies there is an epic battle of good versus evil. The enemy used every device imaginable, catapults, ladders filled with hordes of the enemy to scale the wall, and battering devices to breach the door. In the legendary battle to control the independent city of Troy, the Greeks used a wooden horse filled with soldiers hidden inside to trick them into opening the gate. The people of Troy thought it was a gift. The Greek soldiers snuck out of the trojan horse at night and took over the city. Like the battle scenes in books and movies, there's a battle that wages in the mind for control over these access points.

The story may be fictional, but the ultimate battle between good and evil is epic and true to life in many ways.

The enemy attacks came in waves. In my personal experience, the first assault or wave was isolation. I was separated from my mother at birth and raised as an adoptee. I was in high school before I ever remember my family saying that they loved me. I never felt like I truly belonged. The second wave came in the form of verbal abuse. Because of my need to belong, I chased after companionship without any discretion or wisdom. In fact, I tried to remake myself into whatever others wanted in order to belong. This meant I put up with anything just to be "accepted," but I still felt lost. Physical abuse was the third wave. It crippled me in a way that made me seriously doubt myself. Fear was the fourth wave—the fear of being alone and abandoned. Each assault against me reinforced that fear. Then, shame engulfed me in the fifth wave. I felt ashamed of being a single mom, of my bad choices, of where I ended up in life, and more.

When I repeated negative self-talk, I stopped and declared that I was more than a conqueror. The word conquer comes from the Greek word *hupernikaó*[4], which means to vanquish beyond, as in to gain a decisive victory (more than conquer). Wow! The true meaning of this word means that we do not just win because we score more points. We win by a decisive knockout! This is what it means to be victorious in Christ. Decreeing Scripture counteracts the effects of lies from the enemy. Positive, powerful words war against those negative words. Scripture spoken into the spirit realm applies the antidote to the poison (the negative) in the natural realm. As soon as it is administered, it begins to reverse the effects of the poison.

If satan can keep women occupied with the battle, we are not in our rightful place of authority. Breaching walls is the first strategy of the enemy. He seeks a way in. Women must learn to fortify their gates and close open doors. Gates are points of entry: What we see, hear, smell, touch, and taste. There are different "access points" into our lives where words, what we visualize, our thoughts, other people, etc. can act as an entryway into our being. These access points can only be defended properly if the right foundation is established. His intent is to destroy you.

---

[4] Strong's Exhaustive Concordance 5245

Destroy relationships. Destroy our children. It is his nature. Our gates have to be protected and fortified. A watch is to be set night and day. What is your battle plan?

Step 7 - Boomerangs

Be prepared for what I call the boomerang effect. Years after my relationship with Lincoln and Myles, I was living well, enjoying life free of predators. Then, two successive suitors came across my path before I met and married my husband. The first suitor Fisher had none of the noticeable characteristics of a predator. His predatory nature was revealed through spiritual insight given to my mentor.

Dr. Diane said, "I asked God to reveal Fisher's heart." I did not pray this because I thought I was past this phase. All Dr. Diane heard was "Predator." I was surprised to hear this because he was "so nice." She asked me, "What is the difference between a predator and a nice man?"

The answer is "Nothing, but the motives of their heart." Remember a prince and a predator look the same.

Unlike Fisher, God did send Korbin to be a friend. Korbin restored my hope in finding my birth parents. He used his resources to help me find my mom. That bonding experience led to a marriage proposal. However, once his intentions moved outside of God's will from friend to fiancé, he became controlling. The change in behavior confused me because he had been a good friend, and it was obvious that he was sent from God for a purpose. However, God's grace only extended to friendship—not marriage. Korbin was determined that we should be married. I was hesitant.

Thankfully, a friend shared with me another disturbing dream from the Lord. In the dream I married Korbin and lost my identity. He turned into a predator. The message to me was clear. It was time to break off the relationship.

Both suitors purchased wedding rings. One I gave back to the suitor and the other I gave to a charitable cause. Marrying either one of them was not God's plan for me. Consider the wisdom of Matthew 7:6-8, The Passion Translation (TPT), *"Who would hang earrings on a dog's ear or throw pearls in front of wild pigs? They'll only trample them under their feet and then turn around and tear you to pieces!"*

Value your God-given freedom and never go back to bondage. Stay free move forward, and most of all thrive! The word of the Lord in Galatians 5:1 (TPT) tells us how to throw a boomerang back:

A Life of Freedom

"Let me be clear, the Anointed One has set us free—not partially, but completely and wonderfully free! We must always cherish this truth and stubbornly refuse to go back into the bondage of our past."

Step 8 - Never Give Up

One of my favorite motivational pictures is a turtle at the finish line. Its body is behind the finish line but the turtle has its neck extended across the finish line to win. The caption of the photo reads. "Whatever it takes." I love it because it underscores this principal: Persist until you succeed. Set your intentions. Eliminate failure as an option.

Here is an example of how I applied Scripture.

When negative self-talk came to my mind, I trained myself to stop and declare the opposite-- that I was more than a conqueror. The word conquer comes from the Greek word *hupernikaó*[5], which means to vanquish beyond, as in to gain a decisive victory (more than conquer). Wow! The true meaning of this Scripture means that we do not just win because we score more points. We win by a decisive knockout! This is what it means to be victorious in Christ. Decreeing Scripture counteracts the effects of lies from the enemy. Positive, powerful words war against those negative words. Scripture spoken into the spirit realm applies the antidote to the poison (the negative) in the natural realm. As soon as it is administered, it begins to reverse the effects of the poison.

---

[5] Strong's Exhaustive Concordance 5245

Be encouraged by Galatians 6:9, *"And let us not grow weary while doing good, for in due season we shall reap if we do not lose heart."*

Since the experiences I went through are still going on in the world, for *"there is nothing new under the sun"* (Ephesians 1:9), I am recording steps for you so that you can find the same freedom as I did. It is never too late! Every journey begins with a single step. Make your journey official right here, right now. Choose today that you will sign below and take steps to break free.

Seal your decision with your signature today.

Signature: _____

Date: _____

Resources

IPV starts early and continues throughout the lifespan. An estimated 8.5 million women (seven %) in the U.S. reported a form of intimate partner violence in their lifetime and indicated that they first experienced these or other forms of violence by that partner before the age of 18. 3. If you or someone you know is a victim here are resources:

1. Emergency
    If you are in danger, call 911 or the National Domestic Violence Hotline at 1-800-799-7233 or TTY 1-800-787-3224.

2. Beautiful Women of God Seminars, International
    www.dianegardner.com/

3. Computer, Internet use, and texts can be monitored, and data is difficult to clear completely. If you are afraid your Internet usage might be monitored, call the National Domestic Violence Hotline at 1–800–799–7233 or TTY 1–800–787–3224

4. National Domestic Violence Hotline
    www.thehotline.org/
    1-800-799-7233
    1-800-787-3224 (TTY)

5. National Resource Center on Domestic Violence
   https://www. nrcdv.org/

6. *Breaking Invisible Chains: The Way to Freedom from Domestic Abuse*, Susan Titus Osborn, MA.
   Jeenie Gordon MA, MS, LMFT

7. *Wounded by Words: Healing the Invisible Scars of Emotional Abuse*, Susan Titus Osborn, MA

8. *Overcoming the Enemy's Storms: Healing through the Grace of God*, Diane Gardner

9. *Increase Your Capacity to Hear from God: Stop Walking in Presumption*, Dr. Diane Gardner,
   www.drdianeanswers.com/

10. https://www.loveisrespect.org/
    Chat 24/7/365
    Call: 1. 866. 331. 9474
    TTY: 1. 866. 331. 8453
    Text: loveis to 22522

Endnotes

[i] Breiding, M.J., Basile, K.C., Smith, S.G., Black, M.C., Mahendra, R.R. (2015). *Intimate Partner Violence Surveillance: Uniform Definitions and Recommended Data Elements,*Version 2.0. Atlanta, GA: National Center for Injury Prevention and Control, Centers for Disease Control and Prevention.

[ii] Office of Women's Health, U.S. Department of Health & Human Services, womenshealth.gov. June 11, 2018; Accessed at https://www.womenshealth.gov/relationships-and-safety/domestic-violence/; Last retrieved October 2018.

Kanika Kith

Thank you for your parntership!

John & Anne

Dutrey

Thank you for your parntership!

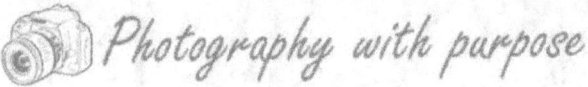 *Photography with purpose*

Killing them softly...
How our media-saturated culture sexualizes
adolescent girls and 3 of the dangers it's causing

Get the free download at:

PhotographyWithPurpose.com

RE/MAX ONE

JOSHUA AND AMANDA
HUIZAR

951-316-5171

Joshhuizar@gmail.com